DREWRY'S *Bluff*

DREWRY'S *Bluff*

LOREE LOUGH

WHITAKER
HOUSE

All Scripture quotations are taken from the King James Version of the Holy Bible.

Drewry's Bluff

Loree Lough
www.loreelough.com

ISBN: 978-1-60374-847-6
eBook: 978-1-60374-848-3
Printed in the United States of America
© 1995, 2013 by Loree Lough

Whitaker House
1030 Hunt Valley Circle
New Kensington, PA 15068
www.whitakerhouse.com

Library of Congress Cataloging-in-Publication Data

Lough, Loree.
  Drewry's bluff / Loree Lough.
    pages cm
  ISBN 978-1-60374-847-6 (alk. paper) -- ISBN 978-1-60374-848-3 (ebook)
  I. Title.
  PS3562.O8147D74 2013
  813'.54--dc23

                    2013008302

1 2 3 4 5 6 7 8 9 10 **ᵾᵾ** 19 18 17 16 15 14 13

Dedication
To my husband, for his support and encouragement,
to my children, for their cooperation
and understanding,
to my Lord and Savior, who called me to write.

PROLOGUE

*Baltimore
Autumn, 1854*

Little Drewry Sheffield missed her mama and papa nearly every minute of every day since they'd died, months earlier. A snake had frightened the roan mares that pulled her father's grand carriage, overturning it and pinning her parents beneath its big, iron-rimmed wheels.

She wished they were here with her now, to explain why she had to sit in this huge room, filled with black-suited, stern-looking men. She hugged her rag doll tightly and met her uncle's clear blue gaze.

"Come sit here on my lap, precious Drew-girl," James said, smiling gently as he patted his thigh. "You look like a scared rabbit, and there's absolutely no reason for you to be afraid."

Drewry snuggled against his big, broad chest. The steady thump, thump, thump of his heart comforted her. "Uncle James," she whispered, "why are we here in this big, dark room? And when can we go home?"

He'd be honest with her; he always had been. She remembered the morning of her fifth birthday, when Muffin disappeared.

Everyone at Plumtree Orchards told her, in sweet sing-songy voices, that her pup had run off to live a happier life in puppy heaven.

But James, seventeen at the time, had waited until the sun was high in the sky, then took her hand and led her along the banks of the Gunpowder River. There, on a ridge overlooking the valley, he told her point-blank that her dog died of distemper. "You're not a baby anymore," he said. "You deserve to know the truth."

She would never forget that. Many times since then, she'd returned to the place Uncle James had dubbed "Drewry's Bluff," since it was there that he hadn't bluffed her about the truth. If only she could go there now!

"What's going on?" she asked again. "Why do they all look so angry?"

"Hush," he soothed softly, patting her slender back. "See there? Mr. Taylor is about to call this meeting to order, at long last."

Dubiously, Drewry eyed Mr. Taylor, a man she'd known her whole life. He and his family had taken dozens of Sunday dinners at the massive mahogany table in the elegant Sheffield dining room. Usually, he had a friendly grin and a mischievous wink for her, but not today. On this bleak, rainy morning, his long, narrow face seemed paler than usual, and the black, bushy brows above his blue eyes were drawn together in a frown. Drewry couldn't decide if he was angry or sad, and couldn't decide why he'd be either....

In fact, every man in the room wore an expression similar to Mr. Taylor's, Drewry noted. Sweet old Mr. Bartell, who snuck her a chip of rock candy each time she stood with her mother at the counter of his general store, wouldn't meet Drewry's eyes. And Pastor Carter, whose friendly smile never failed to produce one of her own, wasn't smiling now. Why, even Mr. Mossman, who always had a red lollipop waiting for her when she went with her father to the bank, was scowling. She felt small and helpless...and very frightened.

Drewry hugged her doll tighter still and squeezed her eyes shut tight. *Sweet Jesus*, she prayed silently, fervently, *please get me out of this scary place!* She held her breath and waited for the magic of God's awesome power to transport her to the cozy comfort of her room. But she wasn't really surprised, when she opened her eyes, to find herself still in the dim, stuffy office....

Her mama had told her time and again that if she was very, very good and prayed very, very hard, the Lord would fill each and every one of her needs. Well, she was as good as she knew how to be. And she prayed harder than she ever prayed in her whole life. Yet God hadn't brought her mama and papa back. Drewry believed His refusal meant she wasn't good enough, hadn't prayed hard enough, to be worthy of His answer.

Joshua Taylor cleared his throat. "I think it's time we get on with the reading of the last will and testament."

The men sat straighter in the red velvet wing chairs that surrounded the lawyer's large oak desk. A rustle of paper whispered through the otherwise silent room as he slid a one-page letter from a white envelope. Drewry knew who had written it, for she recognized the dark scrawl of her father's powerful hand.

"'To whom it may concern,'" the lawyer began reading. "'In the event of the simultaneous deaths of George Ethan Sheffield and Margaret Mary Sheffield, we, being of sound minds and bodies, do hereby instruct Joshua Taylor, trusted friend and attorney, to dispose of our worldly possessions as follows...'"

Taylor stopped, cleared his throat, glanced once around the room. His gaze lingered for a moment on the wide, long-lashed eyes of the child who shuddered involuntarily when he continued reading. "'It is our wish that James Johnson Sheffield shall be executor of our estate and guardian of our only child, Drewry Margaret. All assets and monies now held by First Freeland Bank and Trust shall be made available to him as he deems fit and proper to ensure the financial success of Plumtree Orchard Plantation and all other

Sheffield holdings listed herewith, in order that our daughter shall be guaranteed a secure future....'"

Mr. Mossman inhaled sharply, and Drewry's gaze lighted on him. Why did he seem so upset? Why did he look so very angry?. "What does it all mean, Uncle James?" she whispered, leaning still closer against his broad chest.

"Shhh, Drew-girl," James cautioned. "I'll explain on the way home."

With the unabashed scrutiny of youth, Drewry studied her only relative's handsome face and lively blue eyes. The honesty and affection she saw their eased her mind. Yes, she'd be quiet, because Uncle James had asked her to. She'd do anything for Uncle James.

"Excuse me for a moment," he said, standing. And putting Drewry in the chair where he'd sat, James added, "I'll only be a moment."

Drewry watched him cross to the big, double doors at the back of the room. If he said he'd be back in a moment, then he would. So why did the men look as though they didn't believe him?

James had always been her favorite grown-up. He seemed to understand better than other adults the fears and yearnings of a child's heart. Perhaps it was because he was born a full ten years after her father, and, being the "baby" of the family, was protected from life's burdens and responsibilities, first by his parents and then by his big brother George. Perhaps it was because he'd only recently turned eighteen himself that he lived life like a carefree boy. Whatever the reason, Drewry sensed she could trust her uncle. So, yes, she'd save her questions for the hour-long ride home.

The men who'd gathered to witness the reading of her parents' will moved to a spot near the window. "What was George thinking, leaving his estate in the hands of a ne'er-do-well like James?"

"Now, now," soothed Pastor Carter, "James means well. He's... well, he's a happy-go-lucky sort, is all. Besides," he added, "I don't imagine George really believed James would be taking on such a responsibility so soon."

"You've got that right," the lawyer agreed. "Why, George and Margaret were barely thirty when that carriage overturned." Joshua Taylor shook his head. "Surely they expected to live to a ripe old age…James, too."

Amos Mossman snorted. "He's a hail-fellow-well-met, that's what James is. Why, the boy will likely squander George's entire fortune within a year." He pointed a bony finger at the group. "You mark my words!"

His eyes widened with surprise when he glanced around the room and caught Drewry looking at him. "Goodness!" he whispered hoarsely. "The child's heard every word we've said."

Mossman stepped away from the group and went to Drewry. Crouching, he put his hands on her narrow shoulders. "Drewry, my dear," he said, "everything is going to be all right. You'll see." He gave her shoulders a little squeeze. "But if you ever have a problem…of any kind…come tell me about it, and I promise I'll help in any way I can."

Drewry nodded, but she didn't understand his concern, what "problem" he was talking about, or what "help" could he possibly be, since her Uncle James had promised to take care of her, always…?

Mossman rejoined his cohorts, still huddled near the window. They were her parents' friends. She knew them all her life. So Drewry smiled politely, though their whispers and head shaking sent shivers up her spine.

She searched for her Uncle James, and found him in the outer office, laughing and chatting with Mr. Taylor's pretty young secretary. The minute he spotted Drewry, he sent a merry wink her way, and immediately, a sense of relief flooded over her.

God didn't love her, of that Drewry was sure. He'd proven it when He didn't bring her mama and papa back. She must be a bad girl indeed if even sweet Jesus, who loved all the little children, didn't love her enough to answer such an important prayer. Still, she pondered, she couldn't be all *that* bad…

…not if someone as wonderful as her Uncle James loved her.

ONE

Freeland, Maryland
October, 1868

"Don't you dare contradict me, you ungrateful hussy!" James Sheffield snarled as he raised his hand.

Drewry shrank back from the tall, black-bearded man who reeked of whiskey and cigars. "Uncle James, I can't…you can't…."

"I can and you will!" He let his arm drop heavily when Drewry sprang back out of his reach.

Accustomed to her uncle's drinking bouts, Drewry knew that his intoxicated state would prevent him from pursuing her. This time, however, like a trapped bird, she huddled against the massive walnut sideboard, her blue calico dress and layers of white petticoats billowing about her slender body like a cloud.

"After all I've done for you!" he roared, his words slurring. "Now, don't you go hidin' on me, girl. I need you to save the estate."

"Uncle, I'm grateful to you for raising me, but I will not marry Porter Hopkins," she said, putting as much determination into her words as she could muster. Her body stiffened. "Not even to save Plumtree Orchards."

"He won you as his bride, fair and square."

Drewry felt the bile rise in her throat. "I can't believe you would gamble me away at a poker game, like a cow or a donkey!"

"Believe it."

He lurched toward her again. For the first time in her life, Drewry was truly afraid of her uncle. Seeing an opportunity to escape, she sprang from behind the sideboard, grabbing a heavy, silver soup ladle as she went. Could she use it to defend herself? *Only if I must*, she thought, darting past him and into the butler's pantry.

"Don't come any closer! I'm warning you!" she cried, brandishing the soup ladle like a weapon.

"Sweetheart, surely you don't want your daddy's plantation to go to Hopkins and his good-for-nothin' relatives," Sheffield wheedled, his voice suddenly as soft as melted wax. "Once you're legally Mrs. Porter Hopkins, that ol' coot will give me back the deed, and—"

"Stay away!"

Drewry knew her uncle's drunken tricks. If he couldn't get his way through anger, he sweet talked. Usually, she humored him, listening to his wild ramblings about the War until Old Jeb took him off to bed. Tonight, she was having none of it.

"He's coming to get you at noon. And you'd best be ready—if you know what's good for you."

Suddenly, the red, puffy face of Porter Hopkins flashed before Drewry's eyes. Why, the man practically lived in the saloon! Even the thought of the lout sickened her. She recalled the tobacco juice stains in his mottled beard and his foul, disgraceful language. She shuddered. Marry one of the Freeland's low-life gamblers? Never!

"I won't marry him. You can't make me. I'm nearly twenty-one."

"I can't?" He smirked. "Well, we'll just see about that."

James snatched the key to the dining room door sitting atop the sideboard. In a heartbeat, before Drewry could jump from her hiding place on the other side of the long, narrow room, he stepped outside the heavy door, pulled it shut behind him, and locked it.

As the iron key creaked in the lock, Drewry imagined the sound of a Yankee jailor locking up a Confederate in his cell.

She pounded on the door. "Uncle, for mercy's sake," she wailed, genuinely frightened now, "please don't ask me to marry a man I don't love!"

"Oh, hush your weeping, girl. It isn't as though you have any husband prospects in sight. Just thank God someone will take you."

Drewry slid down the door and crumpled into a heap on the pine wood floor. She crouched there, sobbing into her soft cotton skirts. She shivered as she heard her uncle's brass-capped cane tapping unevenly down the hallway, heading toward the library... and his seemingly never-ending whiskey supply. The eerie sound echoed in the high stairwell as he limped away.

In all her years, Drewry had never felt such deep and utter abandonment. Its icy fingers tightened around her stomach. Her horror at Uncle James's cruelty turned into despair. A raw grief overwhelmed her as she realized he was right: She was alone, and no one wanted her.

Drewry checked the brass timepiece perched on the mantel of the white marble fireplace. Two hours past midnight. How long had she laid there, weeping, before falling into exhausted slumber? She scrambled to her feet. It wouldn't do any good to pray. She knew that by now. And she had wasted enough precious time feeling sorry for herself. If she had any hope of escaping marriage to Porter Hopkins, she'd best hurry.

Drewry eased the window open. The beveled glass panes distorted the bright light of the moon that burnished the dark apple and pear trees in her father's orchards. She lifted her hands to either side of her mouth and drew a deep breath. Moments later an owl's hoot keened over the dusty yard and filtered back to the servants' quarters near the barn. Three times she mimicked the cry—the code she and Old Jeb had been using for years whenever she needed his help with her uncle.

And she had needed the faithful servant's help more times than she cared to remember.

Since returning home from the Civil War, Lieutenant Colonel James Sheffield hadn't been the same. The loving uncle who'd reared Drewry since her parents' death had, for all intents and purposes, perished alongside his men on the battlefield at Gettysburg.

Oh, his body hadn't died, she thought bitterly; instead, it seemed he'd lost his soul. James blamed himself for bad decisions that led to the bloody slaughter of so many Confederates under his command. He came home a haunted man—his hair gone gray, his left foot half shot away, his face scarred, and nearly blind in one eye.

He often woke screaming in the night. Unable to live with the deeds he'd done, he sought solace in the golden elixir of a whiskey bottle, hoping it would hold at bay all the demons that tortured him.

Drewry knew that her uncle had gambled away much of her inheritance at The Silver Dollar Saloon, playing poker with Porter Hopkins and other layabouts who were too busy with drinking and games of chance to tend their crops. Two years earlier, her old friend, banker Amos Mossman, told her that the money her father had worked so hard to earn was nearly gone. "This isn't exactly legal," he'd whispered, thrusting a small sack of cash into her hands, "but I can't in good conscience watch him destroy you *and* Plumtree Orchards." He told her to hide the money…and keep their exchange strictly to herself. Thankfully, she'd taken his advice!

A gentle rapping on the window startled her from her reverie. Peering outside, she saw the familiar form of Old Jeb—trusted friend, farmhand, and former slave.

"Jeb! I'm locked in! He's forcing me to marry Porter Hopkins in the morning!"

"Don't you worry none, Miss Drew," Jeb whispered. "I'll scout out the house and see what Mr. James be up to."

Minutes later, Drewry heard the key in the dining room door. When he opened it, she flung herself against his tall, wiry frame. "Oh, thank the good Lord it's you!"

"There, there," Jeb crooned, patting her shoulders. "The good Lord ain't gonna abandon you in your hour of need. Mr. James be passed out on the liberry couch."

Drewry stepped back and wiped her tears with a corner of her apron. "Will you drive me to the train station, Jeb?"

"'Course I will, Miss Drew. Much as I hate to see you go, you can't marry Porter Hopkins.

"Thank you, dear friend," she whispered, then gave a shudder of revulsion. "I certainly don't want to be a slave of that ol' coot."

"No, ma'am. Ain't right for no one to be owned by another. We is all children of God. Now you go on upstairs an' pack your bags whilst I get the carriage ready."

Drewry threw Jeb a small, sad smile as she slipped out of the dining room. She tiptoed down the hallway, past the library, and up the wide staircase, hardly daring to breathe until she reached her bedchamber.

She dragged her tapestry valise from under the bed and hefted it onto her feather-stuffed comforter. Biting back tears, she threw open the doors of the chiffonier and rooted through her dresses. Velvet, silk, taffeta, brocade—all beautiful gowns, expensive gowns. But she'd have to leave most of them behind.

Quickly, she slipped into a green and gold tartan, a good traveling outfit. She wanted to go far, far away. Far from the fleshy, sweaty hands of Porter Hopkins, far from the terrors of her uncle's post-War madness. She stuffed as many dresses, skirts, and shirtwaists into the valise as would fit.

Next, she opened her rosewood jewelry box, which was empty, thanks to James. Fortunately, she'd hidden a few of the pieces she'd inherited from her mother. There, in the back of her top bureau drawer was the ivory cameo that had come over from England. The ruby necklace and earbobs, a wedding gift from her father to her mother, gleamed in the lamplight. Fighting back tears, she slipped on the jewelry. She didn't want to take any chances on thieves rifling through her valise in the train's baggage car.

Jeb appeared in her doorway, quiet as a ghost. "You ready, Miss Drew?" he whispered.

Almost as an afterthought, she crammed a pair of slippers, an extra pair of button-up boots, and a two-hooped petticoat into the valise.

Jeb hoisted it from the bed. "We'll leave from the gateway so's Mr. James don't hear us…though he be dead to the world, far as I can tell."

As Jeb tiptoed down the servants' staircase, Drewry surveyed the hat-lined shelves in her chiffonier. *I'll wear one and take one*, she decided. Carefully, she placed her best Sunday bonnet in a round flowered box and selected a green velvet hat, decorated with an ostrich feather, for her journey.

At the doorway, she cast one last look around her childhood room. Tears pricked her eyes as she scanned the red velvet window seat and morning chair. She'd never again lounge there, reading romantic stories and the engrossing, melancholy tales of Dickens.

She grasped the thick glass doorknob and quietly closed the door behind her, shutting out the sights of her past. She couldn't bear to look at her grandmother's four-poster bed again. Drewry had been born there, and, all her life, expected that someday, her own children would come into the world in that same fine old piece of furniture.

But it wasn't to be. As the years of taking care of Uncle James stretched out, her girlhood friends married, one by one, and left

Freeland, and Drewry's hope for her own nuptials diminished, like a fading star until, even with a spyglass, a person couldn't see it at all.

~

"Whoa! Steady there, boy!"

Old Jeb's voice soothed the black stallion, who, unaccustomed to pulling the carriage in the middle of the night, was spooked by a rabbit darting across the road.

"Only another five mile' or so, Miss Drew." Jeb turned to his companion in the driving seat and smiled. "We gonna miss you 'round here, Missy an' me. Not that we don't understand why you gotta go...."

Drewry leaned forward and laid her hand on his shoulder. "What would I do without you, old friend?" She swiped at the traitorous tear that slid down her cheek. "Oh, Jeb, what if I never see you again?"

"I'll be 'round, Miss Drew. Folks like you and me, we got a bond, ere." He tapped his thin chest. "So for a while, we'll jus' have to write one 'nother." The old man paused. "It be thanks to your fam'ly that ol' Jeb know how to write at all. Why, if your daddy hadn't taught me, I'd be jus' as ignorant as them other ex-slaves."

Drewry smiled. "Why, he had to teach you to read and write, Jeb. It wasn't right for you to be deprived of the joy of reading the Word of the Lord for yourself."

"Yep." He drew himself up proudly beside her. "Now I reads two chapters from the Good Book each and every day—one from the Old Testament and one from the New. One thing I do know—" he grew serious, turning to regard her solemnly "—you is in the Lord's hands, Miss Drewry. He ain't about to cast off one o' His own. He got plans for you."

Drewry sighed. She wished her faith were as strong as Jeb's. She believed God performed miracles...for other people. But rather than admit how long it had been since she'd trusted in God's care for herself, Drewry stiffened her back and folded her hands over the green velvet purse on her lap.

"You'll have to be careful, Jeb, to see that Uncle James doesn't find my letters. We'll both be in a heap of trouble if he finds out where I am," she said, eager to steer the conversation away from herself.

"Don't you worry none," said Jeb as he slapped the reins against the black horse's back. "I be the one to collect the mail in town. Mr. James ain't done that chore for years." Jeb chuckled softly. "Ain't done none o' the other chores, neither."

Drewry nodded. She knew only too well that Jeb carried the lion's share of running Plumtree Orchards. Silence fell over them for the duration of their trip south from Freeland to Baltimore.

Jeb didn't speak again until she bought her ticket and settled herself on a bench to wait for the early morning train. "Good-bye, Miss Drew," he said, his voice low and gravelly.

Drewry could see tears in the tired old eyes. She reached out and hugged him, an action that earned her a disapproving look from the clerk behind the counter. "Good-bye, Jeb. Take care."

"I'll be prayin' for you, miss. The Lord—He gonna take care of you real good. I know it."

Nodding, she thought, *If only I could believe that….*

Drewry sat near the window in the drafty depot waiting room and peered through the lumpy glass until Jeb's gentle whip prodded the fine black stallion into action. It was a sad moment when the carriage left the train station.

The night was dark as pitch and a moaning wind sighed through the trees. Drewry shivered, though it was an unseasonably warm night. *The Lord—He gonna take care of you real good.* Drewry repeated Jeb's departing words in her mind, vainly trying to draw some small measure of comfort from them. Suddenly, by the light of the flickering oil lamp, she caught her own reflection in the window.

Who was that worried-looking woman?

She tucked wisps of hair under her hat and sat up straighter. *You may be down, Drewry Sheffield, but you're not finished. Not by a long shot. So you were gambled away by your only living relative. You've still got your health, your youth, and enough money to start a new life.*

And where there's life, there's hope....

TWO

It had been the longest, loneliest night of Drewry's life. Sitting upright on the hard, wooden bench at Baltimore's train station, she clutched her one-way ticket like a life preserver. She'd plunked down enough money to take her from Baltimore to Florida…if she chose to go that far. Having never been farther from home than Baltimore, the world seemed as foreboding as it had all those years ago in Joshua Taylor's law office.

From time to time, Drewry's head bobbed as she stole a moment of much-needed slumber. But each time she dozed off, she snapped awake, blinked, and shook off the drowsy feelings. *Can't sleep now*, she told herself. *Not here with these carpetbaggers milling about.*

She heard the mournful whistle of her escape vehicle as it chugged down the tracks. Collecting her overstuffed valise and hatbox onto the boarding platform, the heels of her black boots clicked on the polished marble floors. Fear and excitement knotted her stomach as she stood alone among the crowd on the platform, waiting for the big, black engine to grind to a steaming halt.

"This train's goin' south," the conductor called, leaping from the first passenger car. "Those goin' south...all abo-o-oard!" He stood beside the bottom step, hand extended palm up, to accept tickets.

"Mornin'," he said, nodding as passengers boarded the train. "Watch your step now."

Drewry placed her bag alongside others that would soon be stowed in the baggage car, and said a brief, silent prayer—in case God was listening—that what she'd packed would arrive safely at her destination. The few essentials she stuffed into her suitcase were all she had to call her own now.

"There's a couple of window seats left in the second car," the conductor whispered as she handed him her ticket. "You look like a young lady who wants to see where she's goin'."

She gave him a halfhearted grin. "Thank you, sir." Drewry's voice wavered slightly, and she bit back bitter tears. Thanks to her uncle's latest shenanigans, she had no idea where she might be headed, or what might be in store for her once she arrived there. She had enough money in her drawstring purse to last six months, seven, if she spent every dollar wisely. There wouldn't have been a need to live quite so frugally if she hadn't given Jeb half the money the banker had told her to hide; if her uncle's temper got the better of him, the poor man would need it every bit as much as she did.

When she finally did decide on a place of residence, Drewry would find a job, though she had no idea what sort of work that might be. She'd helped Jeb run the plantation, keeping the books, and she nursed Uncle James back to health. But if a prospective employer demanded a letter of reference....

Before Drewry knew it, she was walking down the narrow carpeted aisle of the train, pressing the green velvet drawstring of her small purse protectively against her waist. A lady nodded as Drewry passed. A gentleman tipped his hat. Since Drewry wasn't inclined to make friendly conversation at the moment, she walked wordlessly to the back of the car, nearest the doors that connected it to the next, and settled into the cushioned window seat against the wall.

With a sinking heart, she realized that she packed in such a rush that she hadn't thought to bring a book or her embroidery or anything else, for that matter, to keep her hands and mind occupied during the trip. How on earth would she pass the time as she headed south!

For the time being, she fussed with the folds of her skirts so that its hem rested neatly atop her black-polished high-heeled boots. For an instant, she wondered if she remembered to toss her button hook into her valise—getting the high-button boots off and on again would be a chore without it—

"Goodness gracious sakes alive!" said the young woman who stood before her. "I hope I'm around to catch you when you swoon. It's sure to happen, ya know, 'cause all bundled up in those frilly clothes the way you are, you're sure to sweat like a pig."

The blonde flopped in an unladylike heap onto the seat across from Drewry's. "I do declare! Don't believe I've ever seen a warmer spring day, have you?" She fanned her face with one ungloved hand.

Drewry's tight-lipped smile, she hoped, would convey to the girl that she should find another seatmate. One far more inclined to idle conversation.

"My, my," she tried again, "looks like you've just swallowed a mouthful of wormy apple!" Giggling, she added, "You're not a day older than me, I'll bet, so why on earth do you look like you've got the weight of Old Father Time on your shoulders?"

With that, she reached out and lightly smacked Drewry's knee. "Smile, for goodness sake! Didn't your mama ever tell you that frownin' makes you old and wrinkly before your time?"

Her mama hadn't taught her much prior to her death, Drewry thought sadly. It had been Missy, Jeb's wife, who'd taught her to behave like a proper lady. Still, Drewry couldn't help but return the girl's grin. She extended her gloved hand. "If we're to be traveling companions, I suppose introductions are in order. My name is Drewry Sheffield."

The girl moved Drewry's arm up and down like a pump handle. "Pleased to meet ya! I'm Suzie Quantoserra." She leaned forward and whispered loudly, "They call me Suzie Q for short."

"Pleased to meet you, Suzie." Drewry plucked her hand from the girl's tight grasp. "What's your destination?"

Suzie rolled her green eyes heavenward. "Richmond, Virginia," she said, frowning, "where I'll mind a rich old fella's motherless brats." She slumped against the seat back, feigning exhaustion. "I'm supposed to meet them at the Richmond station."

She sighed heavily. "The lady at the employment agency wrote Mr. Fancy Pants that I have years of experience rearin' other folks' young'uns." She leaned forward again and whispered conspiratorially, "Truth is, I spent a few months helpin' my sister after she birthed twins." Snickering, Suzie sat back. "But I guess what he don't know won't hurt him, right?"

Drewry inhaled sharply. Suzie barely knew her, yet she had just freely admitted that she not only lied to the employment agency, but planned to continue the charade when she met her future employer! Having grown up without parents herself, Drewry's heart ached a little for the two motherless children, innocently awaiting Suzie's indifferent brand of care.

"Oh, now don't go gettin' all misty-eyed on me," Suzie said, as though she could read Drewry's mind. "Why, those folks have got so much money, they could burn it all winter to keep warm and still not use it all up. Never any need to pity the rich, I always say."

"But, Suzie, those children have no mother."

Suzie rolled her eyes again. "Really, now, you can't be serious. What a mama can't give 'em, their money can buy."

Drewry blinked once before replying, her voice soft and husky, "It can't buy them what they need most…love."

Without a moment's hesitation, Suzie waved the idea away.

"Tish tosh, all those young'uns want is somebody to wait on 'em hand and foot. Well, I'll see to it they don't go 'round thinkin' they're better than others, just because their daddy has more dollars in the bank than most folks. 'Spare the rod and spoil the child,' the Bible says."

The happy light that glowed in Suzie's eyes burned hot and angry now. What awful thing had happened to her, Drewry wondered, to turn her so sour on life at such a young age?

"You can teach them far more with love and kindness," Drewry said, "than you can with harsh words and spankings."

"Hoo-boy! So, Miss Frilly Duds has a temper, has she?" Laughing, Suzie smacked Drewry on the knee again. "Don't get all lathered up now, sweetie. I was just funnin' with you. I ain't gonna waste any of my energy on those brats, I can promise you that. I'll do exactly what Mr. Fancy Pants tells me to, and not one whit more." She jerked her head emphatically.

Just then the conductor sang out, "All abo-o-ard that's goin' aboard!"

A moment later, the hissing, chugging train lurched forward. Steam rose from the engine and floated back over the cars that trailed behind it, temporarily fogging Drewry's vision of the platform. Suddenly, she desperately needed a last look at the Baltimore station, at the tall, gray-walled building and the narrow walkway where Jeb had said his final good-bye. At the road alongside it that led him out of her life, perhaps forever. At the streets and buildings where she'd followed her parents—and her Uncle James in happier days—to see to family business.

But by the time the smoke cleared, the station was out of sight. Hot, bitter disappointment burned in her heart. Very likely, she'd never see this town again. Not if marriage to Porter Hopkins came with the trip home!

⌐

Drewry kept her eyes closed until she felt certain they left Baltimore, and its memories, behind. Only then did she open them to peer through the window at the rolling hills of Maryland's farmland.

"This seat taken?"

Drewry glanced away from the passing landscape and in the direction of the masculine voice. A soldier, standing at attention, stood in the aisle, his slanting blue eyes fused to Suzie's flirty green ones.

The girl slid nearer the window and patted the empty space beside her. "Set yourself down, why don't ya, and take a load off?"

Grinning, he removed his navy blue cap and sat down beside Suzie. "Name's Williams," he said, his right hand forming a proper salute. "Sergeant Duke Williams."

Drewry needn't have worried what she'd do to pass the time between Baltimore and her new mystery home. For the next hour, she listened as Suzie and Duke chattered like a couple of chipmunks.

As they talked, completely absorbed in one another, her mind wandered, from thoughts of her happy childhood with Uncle James, before the War, to thoughts of the hard work and long hours it took to maintain the plantation during his absence.

She hadn't minded adding "nurse" to her long list of daily duties when he came home from battle with a scarred body, mind, and soul. At first, the prayers she prayed beside his sickbed were for his survival. When it became evident that he would live, she beseeched God to help her uncle accept his fate. The left side of his handsome face had been scarred by shrapnel, his left eye partially blinded by a chip of the metal, and half of his left foot had been blown away by a cannonball.

Self-pity was an ugly thing, Drewry realized as she watched her once-lively uncle descend deeper and deeper into the dark abyss of despair. "It's not that I'm vain," he told her once as he waited for the whiskey, prescribed as pain medication by the doctor, to take effect. "But Drew-girl…how will I get by? How will I live my life, now that I'm no longer a whole man?"

She tried to explain that he was the same man…inside. But he wasn't convinced.

"Because of me, dozens of young men are dead," he said, bitter tears punctuating his confession. "I sent them to their deaths. I never deserved more brass buttons on my uniform than they had. I didn't deserve to survive…."

Her prayers, by this time, changed completely in tone and intent, for as the days passed and his physical pain decreased, her uncle's mental anguish increased, and Drewry wondered if he'd ever heal emotionally.

James fashioned himself a gnarled cane. It seemed that with each painful, halting step, his inner turmoil grew. Her prayers now were simply that he'd reach inside himself and find some semblance of the man he used to be. Drewry missed his sweet smile, his teasing jibes, his hearty laughter and his zest for life. She missed his bear hugs, the way he whistled as he moved about the house and grounds, the way he hummed as he trimmed his neat, dark beard every morning. She missed the mischievous gleam in his crisp, blue eyes, and the quirky smirk that slanted his mustachioed mouth. She missed being able to count on him to be there for her, to protect and care for her, as he promised all those years ago in Joshua Taylor's richly-appointed office. Most of all, she missed believing in her Uncle James's unconditional, unstoppable love.

It seemed the harder she prayed, however, the worse James behaved. Self-pity quickly turned to self-blame, and then to self-loathing. In fact, he seemed to find peace only when basking in the golden glow of whiskey. He gambled and cursed and spent money like water. This once kindhearted man now thought nothing of slapping employees about and yelling insulting epithets at his business associates. And though he never actually carried out a threat, he even took to intimidating Drewry with physical violence.

Stubbornly, she clung to the hope that, if she believed strongly enough, the man her uncle had been before the War would come back to her. She dared not send such thoughts heavenward any longer, however, for by that time, Drewry believed herself unworthy of God's ear. And why would she believe otherwise, when not one prayer she'd ever prayed had been answered?

Instead, she went about doing all that was humanly possible to make her beloved uncle comfortable, though he usually fought her every step of the way.

She withstood his hateful words, cried herself to sleep too many nights to count, grieving for the loss of yet another loved one (for Uncle James, as she knew him, was certainly gone). This marriage-to-Porter-Hopkins fiasco, she believed, proved that she'd lost him for good, and that hurt worse than any disappointment that had come before it.

A sudden flurry of activity roused Drewry from her melancholy thoughts. "We're off to the dining car," Suzie announced, clinging possessively to Duke's arm. "Wipe that mournful look off your face, and maybe we'll let ya come with us!" She looked to her companion for approval.

With a quick nod and a friendly grin, Duke added, "We'd be honored if you'd join us, Miss Drewry."

I shouldn't, she told herself. *But I'm hungry.* If she didn't go with them now, she'd have to eat alone later. And since she'd probably be spending countless hours alone in whatever town she decided to make her new home, Drewry decided she'd best take advantage of what might well be the last offer of friendship she'd hear in a long, long time.

She rose slowly and gave as much of a curtsy as the tight space would allow. "Thank you for inviting me," she said quietly.

"Oh, it wasn't nothin'," Suzie said, waving away Drewry's gratitude. "Just don't knock over a teacup and embarrass me," she said, giggling over her shoulder as she led the way down the narrow aisle.

Drewry followed the couple. *She's right. You'd bettertake care not to spill anything,* she told herself, *because there aren't many things to wear in place of this dress if you do!*

Drewry returned to her seat long before Duke and Suzie, feeling the couple wanted a few minutes alone before Suzie was to disembark in Richmond. Drewry stared at the changing scenery, amazed that the weather could so effectively mirror her mood. A steady, unrelenting rain pelted the glass, each drop sliding to the windowsill before disappearing. Thunder rolled and lightning sliced the slate-colored sky as Drewry's spirits continued falling.

Suzie wouldn't get much of a welcome in Richmond, Drewry realized, if the storm didn't let up. But then, she didn't deserve much of a welcome, considering what she intended for the unsuspecting widower and his innocent, motherless children.

The girl was six, Suzie had said, and the boy just three. Their mother, the agency told Suzie, died giving birth to the boy. Mr. Fancy Pants, as Suzie insisted on calling him, tried to be both mother and father to his children and succeeded through that first year. But now that his housekeeper was growing older and his farm was getting bigger, he simply couldn't continue as before. Drewry felt a pang of pity for the elderly gent. Surely he'd be sorely disappointed in the flighty young girl the employment agency had sent to care for his children.

Suzie, Drewry decided, was an odd blend of silly and smart. "Crazy like a fox," Jeb would have said if he met the brassy young woman. She was wearing a blue satin dress with a low-cut bodice—totally inappropriate for day wear and completely wrong for traveling. Nor was Suzie wearing gloves or a hat. Her loud, brash voice was further proof that the girl hadn't been properly schooled in ladylike deportment.

During dinner in the dining car, Suzie's table manners were atrocious. When Drewry pointed out the lovely polished brass lantern on the starched white tablecloth, Suzie merely stared at her reflection in it and fluffed her blond curls. And when Drewry commented on the precise stitching in the ceiling-to-floor velvet draperies and the thick gold-tasseled cords that held them open across the window, Suzie stuck her fingers into the thick, soft folds…leaving a buttery stain behind!

"Next stop, Richmond," the conductor announced, interrupting Drewry's musings.

"Excuse me, sir," Drewry said. "Would you happen to have the time?"

The lanky man pulled a gold watch from his pocket and popped open its lid. "Fifteen minutes before one o'clock," he said before snapping it shut again. "Somebody meetin' you in Richmond?"

Drewry shook her head. "I'm not getting off at this stop, but my seatmate is."

"Then would you like me to hunt you up a pillow? Looks like you could use some sleep."

Drewry smiled at him. "Perhaps later, but thank you just the same."

The conductor nodded and tipped his hat, then disappeared into the next car. In a moment, the train ground to a halt.

Drewry stared out the window at the expectant faces of the people on the platform. Among the dozens of individuals, all scanning the windows for a glimpse of their relatives and friends, one small group stood out: a tall, well-built man with a big, black umbrella was holding tight to a small boy. The man leaned forward, as if checking to make sure the boy still grasped the little girl's hand. Then, satisfied, it seemed, with what he saw, he straightened again and watched as the passengers disembarked.

Suzie and Duke returned just then. "Oh, goodness gracious me!" Suzie exclaimed, peering out the window. "If it isn't Mr. Fancy Pants!"

"How can you be so sure?" Drewry asked, since the girl never met him.

"The lady at the agency said he'd be wearing a blue silk tie, so's I'd know him when I blew into town."

Drewry glanced back at the platform. The man did, indeed, have a blue tie knotted at his throat.

"I sure hope this rain lets up," Suzie said, "'cause I'd hate to leave 'em standin' there, gettin' all wet."

Drewry smiled. "They'll only be out there a moment more. Once the porter finds your bags, you'll all be on your way."

Suzie giggled and snuggled closer to Duke. "We have a little announcement to make, don't we, honey?" she said, kissing the soldier's cheek. "We're getting off in Richmond, all right, but only long enough to find a preacher!"

"A preacher!" Drewry's brown eyes widened in disbelief. "You don't mean to say that in the little while I was gone—"

Suzie beamed. "Yes, indeedy. We've discovered we have a lot in common, and Duke here has asked me to be his bride!"

Duke smiled shyly. "And lucky me, she said yes."

Drewry couldn't believe her ears. How could anyone come to such an important decision so quickly? "But…but what about—"

"Mr. Fancy Pants?" Suzie supplied. "Oh, tish tosh, he'll be just fine. He'll write a few more letters, and before you know it, he'll have another slave girl lined up to watch over his brats." She shrugged unconcernedly.

Drewry looked at the man again, at the expectant expression on his face, the stiff way he held his broad shoulders, and the worry lines creasing his handsome brow. "You can't just leave him there, waiting, with no explanation."

"Just watch me!"

With that, the couple headed down the steps, and arm-in-arm, they faced the train. When Suzie spied Drewry's face in the window, she grinned and waved. "Bye-bye," she mouthed through the glass.

Suddenly, Drewry had an idea. She could get off in Richmond, after all. She could walk right up to Mr. Fancy Pants and introduce herself as the nanny he sent for. The agency hadn't given him a description, Suzie explained, hadn't even given him a name.

Drewry had never done a dishonest thing in all her life, but then, never in all her life had she been in a situation like this one. Right now, a little deception seemed a justifiable, even necessary, means to an end. Uncle James had sold her to Porter Hopkins to secure his future of drinking and gambling, and no doubt her uncle—or worse, Porter Hopkins himself—would come looking for her. Surely, though, they'd never think to search for her on a southern plantation, working as a nanny!

In Drewry's mind, it was the perfect solution to both her problem and that poor man's. And it wasn't as though she'd mislead him about everything—only about the fact that an employment agency sent her to Richmond to look after his children.

She would look after them far better than Suzie planned to! The sight of the children, staring expectantly at the train, tugged at her heart. How well she knew the pain of growing up without a mama!

Her decision made, Drewry gathered up her skirts and hurried from the train. As she stepped down onto the platform, she said a quick prayer of thanks that the rain had let up, leaving out her confession of wrongdoing. She'd tend to that later.

As her eyes met his, Drewry's stomach lurched. *This lie would certainly be easier to tell if the man were fat and bald,* she told herself. *How will you look into that handsome face and…*

Just then, he waved. She nodded to acknowledge his greeting, then stepped over briskly to join the little family.

"Chase Auburn," he said, smiling and extending the hand that had, until moments before, held his little boy's. "And you must be our new nanny."

Her hand trembled as she placed it tentatively into his. "Drewry," she said matter-of-factly. "Drewry Sheffield."

"This is Sam," Chase said, patting his son's dark head. Ruffling his daughter's blond curls, he continued the introductions. "And this is Sally. Say hello to Miss Sheffield, children."

"Hello, Miss Sheffield," the little boy parroted, clinging to his father's arm.

"Hello, Miss Sheffield," the little girl echoed, taking a step closer to her father's side.

Drewry's heart melted. In the wide-eyed gazes, she read fear and uncertainty. Who was this stranger who would be assuming control of their young lives? Would she be kind, or harsh? Suddenly, the lie was the last thing on Drewry's mind. She simply wanted to reassure these frightened little ones.

Stooping to make herself child-sized, Drewry took each of their hands in her own and smiled warmly. "Sam and Sally, what lovely children you are."

"Thank you, Miss Sheffield," they said in unison.

Drewry laughed softly. "Would you mind very much calling me Drewry? 'Miss Sheffield' is quite a mouthful."

They looked to their father. At his approving nod, they grinned. "Doo-ree," said little Sam.

It warmed Drewry's heart to see the fear fade from their eyes. Gently, she squeezed their little hands. "I'll take good care of you," she said. "I promise."

And she aimed to do just that.

THREE

Chase Auburn had not expected such a comely woman to arrive to serve as his children's nanny. Actually, when he thought of it, the word beautiful was a more fitting description of Miss Drewry Sheffield. Slight of build, the top of her head barely reached his shoulder, despite being piled high with thick dark curls. Her skin was the color of milk, and those eyes—wide and longer-lashed than a doe's—though travel-weary—spoke of her intelligence. Yet, looking into those sad brown eyes, he sensed something more.

But what sadness could burden one so young?

Neither had he expected the Baltimore employment agency to send someone whose clothing and mannerisms told of a background of elegance and refinement. Just what kind of girls were taking to nannying children these days! Well, he reminded himself, since the War, many a family fortune was lost. Surely that fact alone made it necessary for some young ladies of good breeding to find ways to earn their own money. But rather than ask potentially distressing questions, Chase concentrated on making his lady nanny feel welcome, especially now that Matilda's advancing age made the daily care of small children a painful exercise.

On their way to the carriage, he quietly observed as Miss Sheffield chatted with Sam and Sally. She commented on Sally's rag doll, saying that she'd had one very much like it as a child. She asked Sam if he knew his letters yet. Under her tender attention, the children's faces seemed to blossom—almost magically—like two upturned sunflowers. Amazingly, although his children were always shy and reserved around strangers, each now had a firm grip on one of her hands.

Chase dug his own hands deep into the pockets of his coat and touched the small ferrotype of Theresa he always carried. Deprived of their own mother, the children craved a motherly presence. Assured by the comfortable chatter between Miss Sheffield, Sam, and Sally, Chase sighed and offered a silent prayer of thanks. He'd had his doubts about sending for a nanny, sight unseen, but he trusted his heavenly Father to provide the perfect one for his family.

"You must be tired, Miss Sheffield," he said as he took Drewry's white-gloved hand and helped her into the carriage. He caught the distinctly feminine fragrance of lavender and smiled. "Please make yourself comfortable. We should reach Magnolia Grange in just over an hour."

Seconds later, a black porter loaded her bulging valise and hatbox into the luggage compartment at the rear of the carriage. Chase tipped him handsomely.

"Thank you, Mr. Auburn, sir, but this be too much money."

"Not at all, Patrick. 'The workman is worthy of his hire,' remember?"

The young man beamed gratefully. "Yes, sir. G'day, sir." He inclined his head respectfully and strode back to the train.

"Before the war, Patrick was a slave on a neighboring plantation," Chase explained as Drewry tidied her skirt and loosened the green velvet bow of her hat. "He was a beaten man back then. Just look at him now! Dignity and self-respect are powerful forces."

"Yes, indeed," said Drewry, flashing a smile that warmed his lonely soul like sunshine melting ice on a pond. He didn't know why her approval should evoke such a curious feeling of pleasure, but a tremor of excitement coursed through his blood...even if tinged with guilt.

In fact, the young woman's sweet smile put a spring into Chase's step as he climbed into the driver's seat and gathered the reins into his leather-gloved hands. Her delicate scent, the light touch of her hand, the gentle tone of her voice filled his senses. He knew, of course, that forever mourning his beloved Theresa wouldn't bring her back, but was it right to take such pleasure in the company of another woman? Desperate to shake the forbidden images, he slapped the reins across the backs of his pair of roan stallions.

Well, at least his children were more content that they had been since the Lord had called their mother, Chase thought as he listened to the hum of their voices. And as the horses' hooves clattered along the cobblestone streets of Richmond, he consciously turned his heart to prayer, echoing Job's words: *"The Lord giveth and the Lord taketh away. Blessed be the name of the Lord."*

∽

Drewry remembered riding in a buckboard when, as a small girl, she accompanied Jeb to Fells Point for supplies. Many times, she'd been a passenger in her father's surrey, a fancy, gold-fringed affair with a high, bouncing seat and big metal wheels. But never in her life had she been conveyed in a carriage as grand as Chase Auburn's!

The entire chassis, jet black and gleaming, was richly trimmed in the same polished brass that adorned the two beveled-glass lanterns mounted up front. Hand-turned wheels with gently tapered spokes were secured by bright red cotters. Drewry couldn't be sure if the ride felt smooth because of the great size of the wheels or because of the springs that allowed the buggy itself to bounce ever so gently with every clip-clop of the horses' hooves.

Red leather seats, tufted and overstuffed, reminded her of the thick feather mattress on her bed at home. *If this is any indication of what I'll see when I arrive at Magnolia Grange,* Drewry thought, *my new home will be quite grand indeed!*

She looked down at the children, snuggled up to her on either side. Her heart ached for them. In those first, lonely years after her parents' deaths, and before the War took her Uncle James, too, Drewry blossomed under his loving ministrations. And old Jeb's wife, Missy, despite having been born into slavery, knew what was required of a proper lady, and taught Drewry to conduct herself with grace and dignity.

It was at Missy's knee that Drewry learned to sew and crochet and embroider. It was Missy's hands that guided hers on the ivory keys of her mother's baby grand. It was Jeb who taught Drewry the soft, soulful melodies that soothed many a sad moment, and Jeb whose gentle advice explained away unkind words and deeds. Drewry decided right then and there that Mr. Auburn's children would receive the best of everything she'd learned from Uncle James, Jeb, and Missy.

Her heart ached for Mr. Auburn, too. The death of his wife must have cost him a huge chunk of his heart. Oh, he smiled a wide, friendly grin, all right, but Drewry noticed that his smile never quite managed to light those dark brown eyes. Perhaps his grief was akin to the way she'd felt when Uncle James returned from his final battle, changed—overnight, it seemed—from the loving man he was before.

Surely, each and every time he looked into the eyes of his children, Mr. Auburn was reminded of his wife. Drewry prayed for the strength to help ease his burdens, as well as to be a good nanny to his children. Because, if the truth be told, she liked Chase Auburn, liked him a bit too much, perhaps, considering they'd only just met.

She sensed great strength in this man. No doubt he could heft a hundred-pound sack with ease. But it was strength of character that ebbed from every pore, and that kind of strength, she knew, was rooted deep within his soul.

Halfway through the ride from Richmond's rail station to the plantation, the children fell asleep. Drewry closed her own eyes, mostly so that she could picture their father in the privacy of her imagination.

He was a striking man, by anyone's standards. Tall and well-muscled, his broad shoulders and narrow waist proclaimed his masculinity. Still, it was his face that intrigued her most. Dark brows arched above near-black eyes, and when he looked at her with that penetrating gaze, it seemed he could see all the way into her very heart. His easy grin revealed even, white teeth.

Drewry's thoughts circled round and round the handsome man who would be her employer. What were the chances, she wondered, that someday he would be more? What would it feel like to be encircled by those powerful arms? And how would her lips respond to a soft, sweet kiss from those well-shaped lips?

Suddenly Drewry's eyes opened wide. *The very idea!* she scolded herself. *You're a hired hand—an employee, and nothing more. And, what's worse, you're here under false pretenses! Get those silly, romantic notions right out of your head, or you're sure to bungle this job even before you begin it!*

Drewry couldn't seriously entertain thoughts of a romance with a man like Chase Auburn. *Why would a man like that want you, Drewry Sheffield, a girl whose only relative thought so little of her that he gambled her away like a meaningless possession? A girl too unworthy even to have her prayers answered?*

It wasn't that Drewry was angry with God for His silence. At least, not anymore. With each passing year, she continued to pray for the things she needed, as her dear mother taught her. And every year, when those prayers went unanswered, her faith died a little more, until finally, she learned to get by without seeking God's help. Her present situation was only further evidence that He wasn't about to rescue her from any ordeal, no matter how terrifying—not even marriage to the vile and despicable Porter Hopkins.

As recently as last night, she'd prayed that something, someone, would put a stop to Uncle James's horrible plan. Instead, she'd been forced to escape by her own hand. Jeb helped out, of course. But that didn't count. He was always helping out. So here she sat, with only a few hundred dollars to her name, one valise of clothes and a lone hatbox to call her own, traveling to a strange new place.

Suddenly Mr. Auburn said over his shoulder, "Look, Miss Sheffield, we're nearly home!"

No amount of description could have prepared Drewry for her first view of the plantation. "Our land begins here," he said, pointing.

She saw the neat board fence that outlined the north edge of his property. He gestured eastward, toward the hilly horizon, using his whip handle as a pointer. "See that line of poplars over there?"

Drewry hugged her tiny purse tightly, knowing even before he spoke that Mr. Auburn would tell her that Magnolia Grange's eastern boundary went as far as the eye could see.

She wondered how many acres made up the grand plantation. Hundreds, maybe even thousands. Drewry sighed and glanced at Sally and Sam. With such a large spread to oversee, he could be gone for days at a time, and she'd be alone with his children. It was an awesome responsibility, and Drewry silently promised she'd never let him—or them—down.

She turned to peer through the oval glass window in the back of the carriage. Then, facing forward again, she stifled a gasp, for the view ahead was breathtaking. The long, narrow drive curved gradually left, then right, like a gently flowing river of white crushed stone. Stately magnolia trees lined the entire length of the drive. Pale ivory buds covered each, and Drewry anticipated the delightful scent that would perfume the air once the buds burst into blossom.

As Mr. Auburn slowed the horses, Drewry caught her first glimpse of the house, a mansion grander than anything she'd ever seen. Black shuttered, many-paned windows offset the wide, double doors on the first floor. A dozen tiers of red brick steps led from the drive to the massive portico. Tall columns supported either side of the porch roof, crowned by a second, equally grand porch that had been enclosed by a white picket rail.

A sense of well-being enveloped Drewry as she looked at the four imposing chimneys, silhouetted against the blue, sun-bright sky. Two gigantic, budding oaks flanked the house. And when Drewry spied the sea of velvety golden daffodils lining the entire front of the mansion, she smiled down at the children, who awoke when the horses slowed their gait.

"Daffodils were my mother's favorite flowers," she said to Sally, whose face was pressed against the carriage window. "What a lovely surprise to be welcomed by them!"

"Papa says they were my mama's favorite, too." The little girl's voice was soft and subdued.

Drewry grasped the small hand and squeezed it reassuringly. "Perhaps we can gather a big bunch soon. Why, we'll put a bouquet on every windowsill!"

Sally smiled and threw her arms around Drewry's neck. Despite the lie that had brought her here, Drewry was grateful that she could fill the empty spot in this little heart.

"Well, c'mon in, child. You must be perishin' with hunger!" Drewry gasped as she found herself enveloped in the arms of a woman as broad as a carriage, or so it seemed. The force of the embrace knocked her hat right off.

"Miss Sheffield, may I introduce my housekeeper, Matilda," announced Chase as he stooped to retrieve the wisp of millinery from the white marble floor.

"P—pleased to meet you, Matilda," Drewry sputtered when finally released from the she-bear hug.

"When I was a lad in knickers, Matilda was my nanny," said Chase, grinning. "That's why I'm spoiled rotten, isn't it, dear lady?"

"The world be hard enough on chil'ren," answered Matilda, "so I says spoil 'em whilst you can. You feel that way, too, Miss Drewry?"

"If by spoiling," she said with a glance at Sam and Sally, "you mean giving them all the love their little hearts can hold, I agree."

"Then we gonna get along fine," Matilda said. "We both got a mama's heart, ain't that right, Mr. Chase?"

He was still holding Drewry's hat when he said, "It's true that you have a mother's heart."

Drewry could hardly blame him for not including her in his compliment. In time, she'd earn his approval.

"Miss Sheffield," he continued, "allow me to introduce the other members of our household." He nodded toward a lithe young girl whose face was surrounded by a mass of fiery curls. "This is Bridget McKenna, our serving girl. Bridget came to us all the way from Cork, Ireland."

Drewry stepped forward and took the girl's hand, surprised by the strength in the slender fingers. "How very nice to meet you, Bridget."

"Oh, but the pleasure's all mine, miss," she said with a quick curtsey.

"And this is our faithful Simon," said Chase, dropping a hand on the older black man's shoulder. "He takes care of the grounds and fixes what breaks in the house."

Simon inclined his head respectfully. His build and demeanor reminded her of Jeb.

"And last but certainly not least, our foreman, Claib. He's the reason we have poinsettias at Christmas, roses at Easter, and orchids all year round. And without him, my crop and hothouse experiments would surely have failed—as predicted loudly and often by our tobacco- and cotton-farming neighbors."

Claib, a brawny man with skin the color of coal, fingered the stained hat in his huge leathery hands. "Miss Sheffield, I hope you'll be happy here. We're right glad to have you."

"Please, you must all call me Drewry," she said. "You've made me feel right at home."

Sally looked up at her pleadingly. "Miss Sheffield...I mean Drewry...Sam and me, we want you to be so happy that you'll stay with us forever."

And she hadn't been with them half a day, yet! Drewry knelt and hugged the child. "Of course I'll stay, sweet girl!" *Until someone catches on to my bluff.*

There was so much more at stake than her own safety. Soon, Mr. Auburn would contact the Baltimore employment agency to assure them of the nanny's safe arrival, and surely they'd write back to tell him that her name didn't match that of the young woman they'd sent. Perhaps she ought to confess, right now, before the children got too attached. Because vulnerable as they were, it would upset them no end to learn the truth....

"Dinner will be ready in an hour," Matilda said. "Enough time for you to freshen up?"

Drewry returned her warm smile. "More than enough." She cast an inquiring glance in Mr. Auburn's direction. "If you'll be so kind as to tell me where I can put my things...."

"Right this way," he said, and led the way up a magnificent walnut-railed staircase. "Anyone living in this house who doesn't feel loved and welcome…well, it's certainly not Matilda's fault," he called over his shoulder.

Claib, carrying her valise and hatbox, agreed.

Their kind words struck Drewry's heart like a blade of cold steel. Everyone at Magnolia Grange had gone out of their way to make her feel a part of the family. But what if someone called her bluff? Who would love her when they found out she'd deliberately deceived them?

FOUR

Upon entering the dining room of Magnolia Grange, Drewry caught her breath, stunned by the splendor of her surroundings.

A six-candle ormolu chandelier cast soft shadows along the red velvet fleur-de-lis wallpaper, highlighted the golden oak sideboard, and glinted off the silver tea service and blue Delft china. The scent of fresh flowers permeated the room.

"Come in!" Chase Auburn, dapper in his black evening coat, strode across the plush Persian rug to take her hand.

A feeling of pleasure coursed through Drewry at his touch and she found herself blushing. "Thank you, Mr. Auburn."

"Please, call me Chase." He winked and nodded toward the children. "We'll be a team, you know."

He led her to the table and pulled out the heavy, leather-backed chair. "I hope you don't mind, but I've asked my other...helpers... to join us tonight in a special meal to welcome you."

Drewry lifted her gaze to meet his. His dark eyes radiated a warmth that made her heart beat faster. *Perhaps I've found a home here, safe from Uncle James and Porter Hopkins,* she thought. *If only...if only I can keep my secret.*

She smoothed the lace trim of her blue calico dress, grateful that she hadn't room to pack her fancier gowns or her six-hooped petticoats; two hoops were plenty for a nanny. Nervously, she brushed back the wide, sausage curls that cascaded down her back, hoping Chase wouldn't think her a silly follower of the latest trends in Godey's fashion plates.

"Of course I don't mind," she said. "I'm a servant, too."

"And I, also."

Drewry shot him a puzzled look.

"Here, we are all servants of Christ," he explained softly.

She nodded, her flush deepening. But Drewry found it comforting that Chase was a man who lived by his convictions. Perhaps he would find it in his heart to forgive her if... Quickly, she cast aside the possibility of being exposed as the impostor she was.

At that moment Matilda brought in a steaming soup tureen. Sally and Sam, dressed in their best, sat swinging their legs impatiently. Claib and Simon were seated side by side, fidgeting a little, as if somewhat unsure of themselves. Bridget, her flaming mane caught up in a black velvet band, helped Matilda serve the meal.

Inhaling the savory aromas of clam chowder, roasted chicken with sage dressing, creamed sweet corn and green peas, and steamed Indian pudding, Drewry suddenly realized how hungry she was.

"Shall we bow our heads for grace?"

As the little group complied, Chase began. "Heavenly Father, bless us, we beseech Thee, and bless this food and the able hands that prepared it. We thank Thee for finding it in Thy will to bring Miss Sheffield to us, for making her part of our family."

Drewry's heart lifted. So Chase was happy to have her at Magnolia Grange! He continued to pray, asking the Lord's blessing on the crops. The humble prayer of this strong man of faith touched her deeply. He spoke quietly, but with an assurance that he was addressing the God of the universe, who heard every word.

Drewry longed to feel such confidence in Him again, to believe that He would hear—and answer—her prayers. To know that He would not reject or abandon her, as her own flesh and blood had done.

"For all these things, we thank Thee, Father, in the name of our Lord Jesus Christ, Amen." Looking up, Drewry found his eyes on her. Quickly, she pretended to be absorbed in undoing her napkin. Even the silver napkin ring told her she'd been accepted here; a well-bred family presented guests with cleverly folded napkins, while napkin rings were reserved for family.

Glumly she placed the linen square over her lap, already regretting the day when they'd learn the truth.

"Drewry, may I offer you some beverage?" With a silver pitcher poised over her cut-glass goblet, Chase quirked his brow. "The good Dr. Hires, inventor of root beer, claims it is one of the best blood purifiers in the world. Says it imparts strength and a clear complexion."

Laughing softly, she held up her glass. "How can I refuse our national temperance drink?"

"It's a favorite in this house," said Chase as he filled Drewry's glass and began filling Sally's. "But, Miss Sheffield, I must warn you that the food here may not be as rich as you prefer."

"Oh?" Drewry eyed the fare. Now that he mentioned it, she did notice an absence of the creamy sauces that graced many tables of means.

"Yes, our Matilda is a devotee of Miss Catharine Beecher's cooking reforms."

"The sister of authoress Harriet Beecher Stowe?" Drewry asked as she took a sip of the cool, sweet root beer.

"The same. Why, her reforms are making as big a stir on gastronomy as *Uncle Tom's Cabin* made in the world of literature."

"What does Miss Beecher recommend?" asked Drewry as she accepted a chowder-filled bowl from Matilda.

"To eat more simply—less flesh, more vegetables. She herself eats no meat. She claims in her books that this diet will prevent the harmful effects of rich foods on the digestion—namely, dyspepsia."

Drewry felt her cheeks redden once more. Speaking of one's internal organs in mixed company was decidedly embarrassing.

Chase seemed to sense her discomfort. "Please forgive me. I quite forgot my manners," he said, his dark eyes concerned. "I'd better watch my tongue, or Matilda will fetch her switch."

"Yessuh!" Matilda said from the far end of the table. She leaned around the steam, rising from the tureen. "Miss Sheffield be a lady, and you best treat her as such."

"Yes, she is a lady," Chase agreed, slanting Drewry an appraising glance. "Tell us, Miss Sheffield, about your home, your people."

She put down her spoon and cast about for an explanation that would protect her identity, while at the same time, would not be an outright lie. "I grew up on a fruit plantation in northern Maryland," she began. "My parents were killed when I was about Sally's age. After that, my Uncle James raised me. Then the War came along and…"

His sad smile brought an immediate softening to the handsome features. "That despicable War caused us all much pain," he said quietly. "Perhaps it's best not to reopen old wounds."

Chase searched her face for a moment, then reached for the bread plate. "Could I interest you in some brown bread? Miss Beecher assures us it's much more nutritious than the bleached-flour variety."

Drewry took a slice and couldn't resist a silent prayer of thanksgiving for this understanding man. She knew God expected truth from His children, but she couldn't help hoping that He would help her keep her awful secret.

Drewry loved her new room. The downy mattress of the big brass bed promised a comfortable night's sleep. When lit, the pair of crystalline lanterns that stood on each round mahogany table flanking her bed flashed thousands of tiny rainbows on the walls and ceiling.

There was not a window seat, like the one in her room at Plumtree Orchards. Instead, French doors opened onto a wide, covered balcony, presenting a spectacular view of Magnolia Grange's northern horizon. The thick, blood-red Persian carpet that covered most of the pine-planked floor would provide protection from the cold when she stepped from bed on chilly mornings. And the maple chiffonier was more than large enough for storing the few dresses she brought from home.

Home....

Snuggling deeper beneath the satiny, down-stuffed comforter, Drewry sighed. Though she'd been gone less than a week, she missed Plumtree Orchards and the scent of flowers that would, by now, be budding on the fruit trees. More than anything else, she missed being able to saunter out to the shed any time she pleased, to find old Jeb stirring a vat of the home-brewed chemicals he invented to discourage the assault of insect attacks on the delicate plantings.

If she closed her eyes, Drewry could see his weathered, friendly face. She recalled how much Jeb resembled her grandfather, Abraham Sheffield. All she had to go on were the ferrotypes she found in a chest in the attic, but the similarities were striking, particularly when Jeb smiled.

She remembered, too, that each time she mentioned the likeness, Jeb's coffee-colored cheeks would darken in an embarrassed flush. "You hush, now, Miss Drew," he'd say, "an' let me get back to work."

It was Drewry's father and Abe's son, George Sheffield, who, despite the dangers of doing so, had taught Jeb to read and write, how to add and subtract, and how to maintain careful control of Plumtree inventory.

On his twenty-first birthday, George's father gave him five hundred acres of rocky bottomland. Abe's thought was that if his son could make things grow in that near-useless soil, he was a farmer, indeed.

At great financial expense, George imported the saplings of fruit trees from South America, the Caribbean Islands, and from as far away as India. At great emotional expense, he endured the scoffing of fellow farmers who expected and predicted his complete and utter failure.

George worked side by side with his hired hands, and within five years, Plumtree Orchards was outproducing Abe's corn and wheat farm. Within ten years, because he had the foresight to add new trees and vines to his product line every season, he was supplying canneries up and down the eastern seaboard with fruits of every variety. And Jeb had been right, every step of the way. "Like brothers, we was," he told Drewry once. "But y'all don't tell nobody I said so," he cautioned, a worried frown creasing his brow.

She'd wondered what worried him, what dark secret he'd been hiding. Drewry understood his fear, now that she was hiding a dark secret of her own. She missed his homespun advice, and yearned to hear again his voice, filtering softly from his room on the third floor of the manor house, crooning sweetly as she drifted off to sleep.

"I'm lucky as I can be to sleep in the big house," he admitted one morning as they sat alone in the kitchen, sipping coffee. "If I wasn't a mulatto, I'd sleep down in the cottages, like the other Nigras."

Not that the other servants were treated poorly; Abraham and George were always good to their hired help, building sturdy houses and giving each a parcel of land on which to plant family favorites. They also provided medical care in time of illness and paid fair wages.

After the War, when all slaves were freed, George taught them to manage their income by allowing them to invest in Plumtree Orchards. When times were good, he gave his help their share of the profits, so that they were able to build up a modest savings. Some bought more land, and others started businesses of their own. Most, however, were content to stay on at Plumtree Orchards, where they were guaranteed a home…and respect.

Jeb always said that he wanted to be buried near Gunpowder River. "So I can hear the water rushin' over the rocks." Drewry made a solemn vow to see that his wish was fulfilled. But how would she keep her promise from way down south in Richmond?

Tears welled in her eyes. Angrily, she swiped them away. "Someday," she whispered into the darkness. "I'll come home someday, Jeb. And when I do, I'll take care of you the way you took care of me ever since Uncle James…"

To finish the thought was a too-painful reminder of Uncle James's transformation. It was as though the grisly sights and sounds he'd witnessed on the battlefield clung to him, and he insisted that the only way he could get any sleep at all was to empty a bottle of red-eye whiskey. Soon, he was drinking in the daytime, too. "Every time I blink, I see 'em, lying all around me," he would ramble between swallows. Before long, Drewry's dear Uncle James was unrecognizable to her. Disheveled and rumpled, he limped about the house and grounds, reeking of alcohol, cursing and complaining at every turn. He became abusive to the hired hands. Abusive, even to Jeb who, thanks to the lessons learned at Abe's knee, was responsible for keeping Plumtree Orchards financially secure.

And Jeb endured it all without a word of complaint. "Why don't you just leave here?" Drewry tearfully asked him after one of

James's particularly violent outbursts. "You're free now. Why don't you just go?"

"Can't," he said in his slow, quiet way. "Who'd look out for you an' the others?"

Drewry sighed. Unable to sleep, she climbed out of the soft bed and tiptoed to the narrow French doors. Outside on the balcony, she hugged herself to fend off the chill of the night air.

Magnolia Grange was a magnificent place. But it wasn't home. Chase Auburn seemed like a kind and decent man, but he wasn't family. Hundreds of times, she'd felt angry with Uncle James, but she'd never hated him, remembering what he was like before kept her love for him alive.

After he frittered away nearly every dime Plumtree Orchards earned, he took to gambling to meet his ever-rising alcohol needs, then sold off most of their lovely furnishings to pay his gambling debts. And when there was nothing worth betting on left anywhere at Plumtree, he tried to hand Drewry over like property, costing her the only home she ever knew and depriving her of her oldest and dearest friend his future, as well.

"Oh, how I miss you, Jeb," she said aloud, biting back bitter tears. "Will I ever see you again?"

FIVE

Drewry didn't know how long she'd been asleep when the piercing screams woke her. She grabbed her thick chenille robe and belted it around her waist as she ran down the hall toward Sally's room.

The child shrieked, pointing to her window. On the grounds below came the sound of horses whinnying, men shouting. A gunshot rang out.

Drewry was torn by indecision. Should she investigate the ruckus or embrace the terrified child? Just then, Sam ran into the room on bare feet and buried his tear-streaked face in the folds of Drewry's robe. The choice was simple—the children came first.

Drewry lifted Sam into her arms and deposited him on the bed beside his sister, then joined the little tykes in the center of the fluffy feather mattress. Drawing Sally and Sam into a warm embrace, she crooned, "There, there, it's all right."

But obviously, it wasn't. The shouts of angry voices intensified. Another gunshot pierced the night. Suddenly, things grew ominously still.

"I'm going to peek out the window to see what's going on," Drewry whispered, "but I'll be back quick as can be to tell you what I've seen." She leaned back slightly and gazed into four frightened eyes. "You'll stay right here?"

Sally grabbed Drewry's hand. "Don't go out there," the child pleaded. "Something bad could happen to you."

Drewry gave her a reassuring hug. "I won't be out of your sight, even for a minute," she promised. She ruffled the children's hair. "Aren't you the least bit curious to know what all the fuss and bother is about?"

Sam nodded. "Is Papa out there?"

"If he is," Drewry said softly, "I'll tell you." She remembered how secure it made her feel when Uncle James had told her the truth about her puppy and the death of her parents.

Drewry scooted off the bed and hurried to the window, being careful to stay hidden behind the curtains. The scene that greeted her eyes was terrifying.

Six men on horseback, each carrying a fiery torch, surrounded Chase. Claib and Simon stood on either side of him, half-aiming their shotguns at the menacing men. Their horses, draped in bedsheets, stomped blanket-wrapped hooves on the gravel drive. Skulls gleamed white in the moonlight and grinned garishly from their resting places on the saddle horns.

The men, in long white robes and tall pointed hats, taunted Chase:

"Nigger-lover! Turncoat!"

The round eyeholes cut into their hoods made them appear even more frightening. "How dare you teach them darkies of yours to read an' write! It's against the law!"

"It's legal now," Chase countered, fists doubled up at his sides. "Now get off my property."

The biggest man dismounted, brandishing his torch. "Where's your loyalty, man?" he demanded. "You're a Virginian, not a

Yankee. Ain't no Yankee law can change how the South feels about slaves."

"Thousands of men gave their lives in the name of freedom," Chase responded. "I'll not dishonor their sacrifice by upholding heathen rituals."

"Heathen!" the giant yelled. "Why, the White Brotherhood follows God's Word to the letter. We're tryin' to save the South, not harm it, you idiot!"

"I've read about your little society," Chase snapped. "You murder and rape and burn, all in the name of Jesus. You're thugs and criminals. A threat to all that's good and decent in the South!"

"We ain't gonna allow nobody to ruin what it's taken more'n a century to build up. Folks like youare the threat, Auburn, with your high-falootin' ways. Teachin' niggers to read an' write, tryin' to grow peas an' carrots where cotton an' tobacco always grew. What are you tryin' to do, man? Where's your respect for tradition?"

Chase stood silent for a long moment, both arms crossed over his chest. "I can't respect any tradition rooted in lies and violence. Now get off my land before I fetch my shotgun."

The big man stood beside his horse. "This here's been a friendly warnin', Auburn. You'd be wise to get back on the straight and narrow...and stay there...or you'll be sorry. You're gonna stop tryin' to make Yankees of us all. You'll pay Old Virginee respect, even if we have to beat it into you!"

Chase reached out and grabbed a corner of the man's robe and pulled. "No man who has to hide beneath a bedsheet scares me. You're a yellow-bellied coward." He looked at the rest of them, one at a time. "You're all cowards. Now for the last time, get off my land!"

The big man leaped into his saddle and signaled his followers. "We'll be going, but this is not the last you'll see of us. And believe me, next time you'll be sorry!" On that note of warning, he spun his horse around and charged down the long, winding drive, his men whooping and hollering behind.

⁓

Drewry, hands over her wildly thumping heart, turned from the window. In the minute that passed as she watched, she could no more deny her fear for Chase than cease breathing. The way he'd stood his ground, unflinching.... The strength of his voice and stance reminded her of the way Uncle James was...once.

But she also feared anew for herself. "I can't respect any tradition rooted in lies," he'd said. How long would it be before he learned the truth about her!

Drewry climbed into the center of Sally's wide bed and gathered the children close. She would tell them the truth, but only as much as they needed to hear, and in language they could understand.

"It seems your father had some...gentlemen callers," she began cautiously, "who don't quite agree with the kinds of seeds he plants. They were trying to convince him that he ought to plant nothing but cotton and tobacco, like everybody else in Richmond."

"But why were they shouting?" Sam asked, his voice trembling.

"Oh," Drewry replied with a nonchalant wave of her hand, "some men just like to make a lot of noise." She gave a little laugh, more for the children's sake than to express any levity she felt. "I guess they want to make sure everybody hears what they have to say."

"They sounded so angry," Sally said.

Drewry pictured the scene. She hadn't needed to see the expressions hidden by those white hoods to know how furious... and determined...they'd been.

"Let's pray for them," Drewry suggested, "so that they'll get a good night's sleep, and wake up happy as larks!"

It was a ridiculous thing to suggest, but since it seemed to calm and comfort the children, Drewry was only too happy to sound silly. Later, long after they were fast asleep again, she'd say a few prayers of her own. Because if that evil man's threats had been heartfelt, Chase would need every bit of protection the good Lord could deliver.

⌢

The moment the riders were out of sight, Chase ran into the house and up the stairs. When he passed Sam's room, the empty bed alarmed him...until he heard his son's voice coming from Sally's room. It was then that he heard Drewry's voice, soft and reassuring, "...I guess they want to make sure everybody hears what they have to say."

Chase leaned against the wall and crossed one booted foot over the other. Despite his recent confrontation with the hooded men, he smiled as he eavesdropped on the new nanny and her small charges.

"Are the men gonna hurt Papa?" Sally asked.

"Your father is big and strong and smarter than all those men put together," Drewry told her. "They're going to have to do a lot more than holler and yell to hurt him!"

She hadn't lied to his daughter, Chase noticed, yet she'd made Sally believe that he was safe from the night visitors' threats.

"They said they'd be back," Sally stated, remembering. "Will they come in the dark again? Will they come soon?"

Chase heard Drewry's long, deep sigh. "Sally, my sweet, I'm sure they won't want to climb out of their nice warm beds!" Then she suggested that they pray for the clansmen. Of all things!

"Where's Papa?" Sam wanted to know.

"I'm right here." Chase strode into the room and stood beside the bed. "Do you children realize that it's past midnight?" He gave Drewry a wink as he gathered the boy into his arms.

Sam rested his head on Chase's shoulder. "Will the bad men come back tonight, Papa?"

"No, son. They won't." *At least, not tonight.* "Now, what do you say we get you tucked into bed?"

"I'll do it." Drewry rose from Sally's bed and held out her arms, waiting for Chase to hand over his son.

He shook his head. "Thank you, but I'd rather do it myself, if you don't mind." Chase walked nearer the bed and leaned over to kiss Sally's cheek. "Good night, sweet child," he whispered. "May the good Lord grant you beautiful dreams and send a legion of angels to watch over you."

"G'night, Papa." Sally smiled sleepily and wrapped her arms around her father's neck.

Straightening, Chase headed for the door, pausing to say, "Give me a few minutes. Then I'd like a word with you in my library, Drewry."

Drewry's heart pounded. *What could he possibly want at this hour?* "Yes sir. I'll be down just as soon as I've tucked Sally in."

Much as she tried, Drewry scarcely heard a word the child said once Chase left the room. Had the agency contacted him to check on the new nanny they'd sent? Would he demand an explanation for her deceit? Would he insist upon her immediate resignation?

As if through a fog, Drewry listened to the little girl's prayers—for the second time that night—and gave her a hug and a kiss, and promised to take her and her brother for a long walk in the morning. But she knew that no matter which direction they went on their excursion, it wouldn't be nearly as long and difficult a trip as her descent down the winding staircase that led to Chase's library.

⌒

Drewry made a quick stop in her own room to slip into a simple cotton dress. "Ain't fittin' nor proper for a young lady to be flittin' about in her nightclothes," Jeb's wife Missy would have said.

"I couldn't help overhearing what you said to the children," Chase began, motioning to her to take the tufted brown leather chair opposite his as soon as she entered the room. "I must say, I was quite impressed with your aplomb tonight."

Drewry breathed a sigh of relief. Perhaps she hadn't been found out, after all....

Chase stood and began pacing the length of the library, his boots thudding softly on the thick Oriental carpet.

"Who were those men?" she asked, wide-eyed.

"They call themselves the White Brotherhood; The Society of the White Rose; The Ku Klux Klan. There are many interesting names for their little...club." Chase spat out the last word as if it were a mouthful of rotted meat. "What they really are is a gang of bullies."

"If their goal is to terrorize, they've succeeded." Drewry sighed. "Skulls and crossbones...torches...muskets...." She shuddered at the memory of the white-sheeted hoodlums. "And those awful, awful masks!"

Chase laughed softly and returned to his seat. "Yes, they're a sorry sight, all right."

"'Ku Klux Klan,'" Drewry repeated. "What sort of language is that?"

"It's Greek, and it means 'circle.' They hope to impress upon us how well-organized they are—impenetrable from the outside, inescapable from the inside. Their symbol is a cross within the circle, to prove they're doing God's work, which is the greatest irony of all. In persecuting Christ's people, they are persecuting the Lord Himself."

Drewry remembered Christ's words to Paul on a similar mission along the Damascus road: *"Saul, Saul, why do you persecute me?"*

Chase settled back in the chair. "When they first started raiding the countryside, their aim was to have us believe they were the discontented spirits of dead Confederate soldiers, out to seek vengeance upon those for whom they died in vain. That's why they hide behind white gowns and hoods."

Drewry leaned forward and hugged herself.

"But enough talk of dark deeds." He held out his hand to her. "Why don't we go into the kitchen and see if there's any milk left from supper. Perhaps you'll warm us both a cup to settle our nerves."

For a minute there, in Sally's room, Drewry feared he'd uncovered her bluff. Now, almost weak with relief, she put her hand into his as he helped her to her feet.

"My old nanny used to float a pat of butter on our warm milk," she said, walking beside him through the quiet house.

"Is that so?"

Realizing that she'd betrayed herself, Drewry withdrew her hand hastily. *You little ninny!* she scolded herself. *You've gone and admitted you were once well off enough to afford a nanny of your own!* "My guardian," she explained carefully, "owned a sizable farm before the War."

"Ah, yes," Chase said, lighting the lamp that hung above the kitchen table. "That abominable War. It cost your guardian a great deal, then?"

Drewry opened the back door, stepped out onto the porch, and reached into the wood-lined iron box where she Matilda stored the pitcher of milk. "Yes," she said truthfully, shutting the door. "He barely escaped with his life."

Chase placed two heavy white mugs on the table, then sat on one of the stools stored beneath it as Drewry poured milk into the copper kettle on the stove. "You said you were quite young when you lost your parents. Did they leave you in the care of this guardian?"

Drewry nodded, then poked the coals in the stove. "Yes. He's my father's brother." In one instant, she saw Uncle James again—tall, dark-bearded, handsome, full of life. In the next, she pictured him as she saw him last—rumpled and red-eyed, flailing his cane like a sword….

"You handled things quite admirably tonight," Chase said quietly. "I'm sure the children were very upset when they heard all the ruckus outside."

"Yes," she admitted, "they were terrified, at first. But I think they'll be fine as long as we're honest with them."

Chase nodded his agreement. "I've always felt it's far easier to deal with fact than fantasy. My dear departed mother—we lost her to pleurisy last year—practically insisted we tell Sally that her mother was not dead, only asleep." He scowled, then added, "When Sam grew old enough to understand, were we to tell him the same lie? And what were the children to think when their mother never woke up? Why, it would make them afraid to sleep, themselves!"

Drewry tilted the kettle left and right to help the milk heat evenly, hearing the hiss. She searched the cupboards for a bit of butter, and found it in a crock on the fancifully carved wood shelf.

"My uncle was quite straightforward with me when my parents were killed. Knowing how they died was easier to bear that wondering why they'd left me. I'm sure my acceptance of being orphaned was a direct result of his honesty."

"And just how didthey die, Drewry?"

She met his gaze, warm and brown and understanding. Grasping the kettle's blue-flowered ceramic handle with a crocheted potholder, Drewry stepped up to the table and filled their mugs. The milk bubbled and steamed, and as the dollop of butter she added began to melt, tiny golden circles floated atop the foamy white surface. She used the butter spoon to stir her milk, then handed a mug to Chase and sat down across from him.

She'd have to tread carefully here—give him enough information to satisfy his curiosity, yet not so much that he'd be able to track down her family. "Mama and Papa went to Baltimore on business," she began cautiously, keeping her eyes downcast. "A snake in the road frightened the horses, and their carriage—"

Chase halted her before she could continue. "I'm sorry, Drewry. I shouldn't have asked." He sipped his milk, studying her solicitously. "So tell me, what do you think of your new home?"

She met his eyes then. "Oh, your house is simply lovely."

He returned her warm smile. Then, wrapping his hands around his mug, he added, "And your room…is it to your liking? We could rearrange the furnishings, or…"

"You're very kind to offer, but I wouldn't change a thing. I'm sure I'll be quite happy here," she assured him. "I'm only hoping that I'll be able to help you make those beautiful children of yours feel content and protected, always."

It seemed to be just what he needed to hear, for the sparkle returned to his dark eyes. He downed the last of his milk, then rose. "It's very late. Perhaps we'd best get some sleep now."

At the door, he paused and glanced over his shoulder. "Good night, Drewry," he said softly. "And thank you…"

She opened her mouth to question why he was thanking her, but he was gone. Suddenly, the kitchen, which had seemed bright and cozy before, now felt chilly. The answer would have to wait until morning. Meanwhile, she'd have to make it through the remainder of this long, strange night…alone. A perfect time, she thought, to write her dear friend.

Magnolia Grange
Richmond, Virginia
March, 1968

Dear Jeb,
I'm sorry it's taken me so long to write you, but things have been so busy here.

You'll be happy to hear that I have found myself a home—at least for now. I met a girl on the southbound train who was traveling to Virginia to become the nanny for a rich man's children. Well, as it turned out, the "nanny" met up with a soldier, and they're married by now, I suppose. So your Drewry assumed her position—unbeknownst to my new employer, unfortunately.

I am in a place near Richmond, Virginia, known as Magnolia Grange, a magnificent plantation owned by Mr. Chase Auburn. He is working on some crop experiments. If Mr. Auburn (he insists I call him Chase) succeeds in getting his soy beans and hothouse plants on the market, he'll be a very rich man indeed, for he'll be able to sell his produce locally and save on the cost of having the goods shipped in.

I have more or less settled into my new home. My, but how grand Magnolia Grange is! You would love the gardens here, Jeb. There are daffodils and tulips of every color of the rainbow in bloom already—imported, I'm told, from Holland. The children say I've missed the crocus season, but tell me that more will bloom in the fall. I expect I'll be here to see those…if my small deception is not discovered first.

If only it were possible for you to meet my delightful charges! Sally is six, and has her father's dark eyes and hair. Matilda (who's the real boss around here), tells me that Sam will be four come November. Sam, says Matilda, looks like his mama— golden brown hair, hazel eyes, and an angel's smile. They're such sweet children, Jeb. Taking care of them is my job I suppose, but it no chore at all. I believe I'm going to enjoy it here very much.

It seems so long since I last saw you. I yearn to hear you sing a sad old ballad. And I sure could use some of your down-to-earth advice. I hope Uncle James isn't making life too unbearable for you and Missy these days. You'll write me soon, won't you, and let me know how you're getting on? Tell me, too, how old Porter took the news that his bride-to-be escaped on the morning train!

Until I hear from you, please know that you're in my thoughts and prayers always.

With my fondest affection,
Drewry

SIX

"What's Sheriff Kelly doin' here?" Matilda asked, peeking through the lacy white curtain in the front parlor. "He's the worst mannered man east of the Mississippi." She stood back and planted chubby fists on her wide-spread hips. "Why, he left his horse right out in the middle of the yard! Now who's gonna clean up after the beast?"

She grimaced when he pounded on the front door. "Dear Lawd," Matilda muttered, waddling into the foyer, "give me the strength to keep a civil tongue in my head whilst he be a guest in Mr. Auburn's home."

Drewry looked on in fascination as Matilda ranted. She listened, more fascinated still as the housekeeper greeted him: "Why, Sheriff Kelly, what you be doin' in these here parts? Seem like ages since I see you last."

Alden Kelly bristled under Matilda's syrupy scrutiny. "Where's Chase?" he demanded. "I need to speak to him, right now."

"Well, sir, do come in," Matilda sang, "an' set yourself down in the parlor whilst I fetch 'im." Behind his back, she rolled her eyes and made a face at Drewry. But her countenance was benign once again when Alden Kelly turned to seat himself on the plush green divan. "Can I git ya somethin', Sheriff? Maybe a cup o' tea?"

"Just get Chase in here," he snorted.

Drewry inhaled sharply, recognizing Kelly's gravelly voice as the one belonging to the leader of the White Brotherhood. She shivered involuntarily and stepped past him toward the foyer.

"Hold up just a minute, there, Matilda," Kelly said. "Who's this pretty young thing?"

Matilda stepped in front of Drewry protectively. "Why, this be Miss Sheffield, Sheriff, Mister Chase's new nanny. She gonna take care of Sally an' Sam. Gonna teach 'em to read an' write an' cipher. Ain't that right, Miss Drew?"

Drewry, thankful for the security of the woman's nearness, nodded.

Kelly squinted appraisingly. "Got a feller?"

"'Course she ain't," Matilda answered for her. "She ain't gonna git no feller no time soon, neither, 'cause Mr. Chase, he be wantin' her to get busy educatin' his young'uns. Ain't that right, Miss Drew?"

Again, Drewry nodded dumbly.

Matilda faced her head on. "Why don't you go on upstairs an' find Mr. Chase, Miss Drew, whilst I put on a kettle of water, in case he wants a cup of tea to sip whilst he an' the sheriff, here, talk."

Gratefully, Drewry escaped up the steps. She found Chase in his library, poring over another of his thick agriculture textbooks. Surprised by her sudden appearance, he looked up and smiled. "Well, what brings you here?" He leaned back in his leather chair. "Haven't seen you since—" he glanced at his pocket watch "—since breakfast, half an hour ago."

Without asking permission, Drewry slid the library's pocket doors shut. "Matilda said that I should let you know you have a visitor." She wrung her hands in front of her.

"Oh?" Chase got to his feet.

"It's Sheriff Kelly. I recognized his voice. He's…"

Chase walked around to the front of his desk and patted her shoulder. "Now, now. Calm yourself, Drewry."

"But he was here last night. *He's* the leader of that gang!"

"There's nothing to worry about. Trust me."

She sighed deeply. "But he's such a vile and vicious man. What if…"

Chase turned and walked toward the door. "Why don't we find out what brought him all the way out to Magnolia Grange this time?"

Drewry's feet seemed frozen to the spot. But when Chase opened the doors and entered the hall, Drewry found the strength to move. She couldn't leave him alone with that horrible man. What if the sheriff threatened him again…or worse? *Well*, Drewry decided, *this time Chase will have a witness!*

"Alden Kelly," Chase said as he strode into the parlor, "what can I do for you this fine morning?"

"I've been gettin' complaints about you, Auburn," Kelly spat, leaning forward in the big armchair near the fireplace. "Folks don't like the way your niggers traipse around town like they own the place."

Chase frowned. "I'll thank you not to use that word in my home, Sheriff."

"What word?" Kelly sneered. "Oh, you mean *nigger*?"

Chase leveled him with a stern look. "I have work to do, Kelly, so if you'll just tell me why you're here…"

"Told you already. No true Virginian likes an uppity nigger. You need to take yours to task."

Drewry stepped timidly into the room and sat as near Chase as the seating arrangement allowed. She squared her shoulders and lifted her chin, then cast a defiant glare in Kelly's direction.

There was a dangerous glint in Chase's eyes as he said, "I wasn't aware that being uppity was against the law."

Kelly shot to his feet. "You've been warned, Auburn. But only 'cause my wife insisted on it. She's a God-fearin' woman who believes every man deserves a fair shake. If not for her, I wouldn't have bothered to come here today at all."

Chase stood, too. "Then by all means, be sure to thank your good wife for me." Almost casually, he glanced at Drewry, who was still sitting stiff and solemn in the chair beside the sofa. "I don't believe you've met the newest member of our family...."

Kelly waved an impatient hand in the air. "Yeah, yeah. Your nigger woman intro—"

"You'll kindly refrain from referring to Matilda in that way," Chase interrupted. "She's the manager of my household, and as such, deserves your respect."

"No nigger deserves re—"

The ominous look in Chase's eyes silenced the sheriff. "Well, if there's nothing more, let me walk you to the door."

At this, Drewry rose, just in time to see Alden Kelly line up with Chase. Toe-to-toe, the men glared at each other.

Kelly was shorter than Chase by at least two inches, but carried at least fifty extra pounds around his middle. *Put there by drink and gluttony, no doubt,* Drewry surmised, frowning in disgust.

"You'd better quit actin' like a Yankee," Kelly said, wagging his stubby forefinger under Chase's nose, "or you're gonna be sorry."

"And if you don't stop abusing your powers, *you'll* be sorry."

"Me?" Kelly's wicked laughter ricocheted off the walls. "Why should I be sorry?"

Chase's eyes narrowed dangerously, as did his voice. "Because some folks around here don't agree with your strong-armed tactics, and if they found out what kind of clothing you wear when you call on your neighbors in the middle of the night, they'd be mighty distressed. You might have a hard time summoning votes in the next election, even if you paid for them, as I'm told you did in the last one...."

Kelly coughed and sputtered, then said through clenched teeth, "You're out of your mind, man. Who do you think folks is gonna believe—the feller who puts his life on the line every day to keep law and order in their town, or some high-falootin' rich man, plantin' Yankee crops? It's your word against mine."

"Sheriff Kelly," Drewry said in a honeyed tone, "I wonder if you could tell me about the emblem on your...costume. What does it mean?"

"Uh, emblem?" He frowned. "What costume?"

"Why, the one sewn on the white robe you were wearing last night, of course."

Kelly scowled. "Women," he puffed, "should be seen and not heard."

Drewry arched her brow. "I've never heard the term 'high-falootin' before, but I heard it last night. And just a moment ago, you said it again. I've never heard a cough quite like yours, either. You really ought to see a doctor. It could be the tuberculosis...."

"What in tarnation is she babblin' about?" Kelly demanded, turning to Chase.

"I believe she's saying that she could testify in a court of law that she recognizes you as part of the gang that was here last night," he replied evenly.

"I...uh...I don't know what you're talkin' about, either of you," the sheriff sputtered. "I think you're both a bubble off plumb, that's what I think!" He jammed his hat back on his head and headed for the door. "Just remember, you've been warned, Auburn," he said, then slammed the door behind him.

Chase and Drewry stood side by side in the parlor, listening as Kelly's horse clattered down the gravel drive. When the sounds of his exit were no longer audible, Chase faced her. "That was a very brave thing you did just now. It means a great deal to know that you're so devoted to Magnolia Grange..."

Drewry blushed, inordinately pleased with his compliment.

"...but I'm afraid it wasn't very smart." His frown disturbed the perfect symmetry of his strong brow. "Alden Kelly isn't someone you want for an enemy."

Stunned by this sudden change of attitude, Drewry faked a brave smile. "Why, I can't think of a single person I would want as an enemy!"

"This is no laughing matter," Chase went on, his tone severe. "The man is insane, along with the crowd that follows him. There's no telling what they might do to spread their message of hatred."

He sighed deeply. "You've put yourself in grave danger, interfering like that, and in so doing, you've also put my children at risk."

Drewry blinked rapidly. "I—I'm so sorry. I didn't realize. I never thought..."

To her surprise, he reached for her and drew her into a protective hug. Her heart hammered as she rested her head on his chest and listened to his soothing words. "I'm sorry if I've frightened you, Drewry. But I had to make you understand that you must weigh every decision you make carefully; everything you do from here on out will, in one way or another, affect my children."

He held her at arm's length. "I understand what you were trying to do, and I thank you from the bottom of my heart for your loyalty. But I can take care of myself. *Your* first responsibility is the children." Chase released his hold and stepped away. "Incidentally, where are the children?"

"They—they're out back, collecting flower petals for a project I have planned for them."

He took a deep breath. "Go to them, then, while I give some thought to how we're going to handle Kelly and his rowdy boys."

Drewry so wanted to take good care of Sally and Sam, and already, she'd failed. "I'm so sorry," she said again.

"Don't be sorry," he said, heading back toward the sanctuary of his library. "Be careful."

He was right. She couldn't deny that. What she'd intended as a good deed had been anything but. Drewry was left—once again—with the inescapable fact that she'd proved herself unworthy.

And if unworthy, then no wonder she was unlovable!

⌣

Claib flicked the whip over the strong backs of the matched horses drawing Chase's grand carriage, and the blacks picked up their pace.

"What you be buyin' in town today, Miss Drew?" Matilda inquired curiously.

"Fabric, I hope. I plan to make Sally a dress for her birthday party."

Matilda nodded. "Only yesterday, she told me she ain't got a proper party dress." She gave Drewry a sidelong look. "Her fav'rite color be blue, you know, same as her mama's."

"Thank you, Matilda. I don't know what I'd do without you to help me care for Sam and Sally."

Matilda drew herself up proudly, her eyes on Claib's back. "L'il Sam, his fav'rite color be red. Like Mr. Chase."

Drewry giggled. "Why, I would have figured Chase for a 'gray' man or even black— something dignified and gentlemanly...."

Matilda slapped her thighs and leaned back, her hearty laughter interrupting Drewry's comment.

"'Tilda," Claib called over his shoulder, "you hush up back there, 'fore you spook the horses, hear?"

Matilda made a feeble attempt to compose herself. "Miss Drew, if you think Mr. Chase be a dignified gent, you don't know him like I do."

Drewry smiled into the broad black face, thinking, *oh, but I wish I did!*

"Mr. Chase weren't no easy young'un to raise," Matilda continued confidentially. "Why, that boy, he could find mischief just about any place. Ain't that right, Claib?" she asked, poking her old friend's shoulder.

"Yep," Claib agreed, snickering. "Mr. Chase was one ornery li'l tike, all right."

Drewry shook her head. "But he's so proper and distinguished. I'd never have believed he could be anything else, even as a boy!"

This time, Claib's laughter joined Matilda's. When the sound died away, the woman grew serious. "Miss Drew, the man you see today is the man Miss T'resa made of him."

Drewry frowned. "His wife? Didn't she like him the way he was?" Drewry found that hard to believe since, in her mind, Chase was the most nearly perfect man she ever met.

Matilda shook her head. "She liked him just fine. But Miss T'resa, God-lovin' woman that she was, took a mind to tame Mr. Chase, and that's 'zactly what she did."

"Made a silk purse outta a sow's ear," Claib agreed.

"Them two were mighty happy," Matilda added thoughtfully. "Why, I never seen a man smile like he done when she say they gonna have a baby." Matilda clasped her hands in front of her ample bosom. "And when she left this ol' world, I believe he cried a bucket o' tears. Ain't that right, Claib?"

He nodded solemnly.

"Hardly touched his food. Barely said a word to nobody, 'cept them young'uns." She sighed heavily. "Then he went back to church, 'cause Pastor Tillman told him he best take control of himself before the children had no mama *and* no papa. So Mr. Chase, he commence to prayin' most all day. It kept him calm enough through the daylight hours. But at night…" Matilda drew an embroidered handkerchief from her handbag and dabbed at her teary eyes. "I don't believe I ever heard such mournful wailin' as what come from his bedchamber. Broke my heart to hear him weep like that."

Claib nodded. "Plumb pitiful, all right."

"I know something about losin' loved ones," Matilda interrupted. "Lost my man while our only young'un was still inside me. Lost that young'un—a Buffalo soldier—during the War. But I never grieved like Mr. Chase. No siree."

While Matilda's sad story moved Drewry's heart, her thoughts turned to Chase. It was hard to imagine that just three years ago, this strong and capable man had nearly given in to his grief. Drewry felt a deep and abiding compassion for him, and a glimmer of hope swelled within her.... They had more in common than the care and well-being of his children. They'd both loved and lost people who had been central to their lives.

"I hope someone will love me that way someday," she blurted out. Then, as if regretting her impulsive words, Drewry readjusted the folds of her skirt and added, "Though I'm aware I'm destined to become an old maid."

"Shucks, Miss Drew," Claib said, "seem to me you're just getting to the marryin' age. Besides, you ain't all silly an' giggly. You know the value of a dollar. And you have a heart the size of all Virginee."

Matilda nodded in agreement. "Not only that, child, but you're as honest as the day is long!"

Drewry felt her cheeks grow pale. Nothing about her life these days seemed honest. She knew that the Scriptures talked about building a house on a firm foundation so as to endure, but her life in Virginia had been built on a foundation of lies. It was only a matter of time before her entire world came tumbling down.

Unaware of her distress, Matilda talked on. "And if you want my opinion, you're a sight prettier than most. Why, any man worth his salt can see that right off."

You've no right burdening these good people with your dreams and wishes, Drewry reprimanded herself. *And if you had one ounce of decency in you, you'd tell them the whole truth!* For an instant,

Drewry considered doing just that. "*Confession is good for the soul*," Jeb used to say...."

But Matilda interrupted her soul-searching. "I'll let you in on a little secret, if you promise to keep it to yourself," she whispered, mischief glinting in her dark eyes.

Curious, Drewry put aside her urge to confess and leaned near.

"Well, I recollect the way Mr. Chase used to look at Miss T'resa before they married. His eyes would shine and he'd stare—till somebody caught him at it." Matilda chuckled softly. "Got all tongue-tied 'round her, too."

Drewry swallowed the stinging sensation of envy that bubbled inside her at the thought of Chase looking longingly at his beloved. She couldn't imagine why she felt this way; he was her employer, after all, and nothing more. Besides, didn't the man have a perfect right to moon over the woman he'd loved?

But Matilda, oblivious to Drewry's dark musings, grinned as she continued. "Mr. Chase likes you, Miss Drew. I can tell."

The only thing Drewry could remember was the gentle scolding he'd given her that morning, after Sheriff Kelly's hasty departure. "Well, I—I hope so. I like him, too. He's a very kind man. And a fine father."

Matilda elbowed Drewry in the ribs. "That's not what I'm talkin' 'bout, Miss Drew. I mean, Mr. Chase *likes* you...the way a man likes a woman."

"True enough," Claib agreed, eavesdropping from his seat up front. "Plenty of times, I seen him lookin' at you in that special way."

Drewry gasped. Were they both daft? They must be! And yet, a quiet note of joy sang in her heart at the possibility that Chase might think of her as more than a mere employee. "I—I don't know what to say."

"No need to say nothin', Miss Drew," Matilda said, the wisdom of her years echoing in her tone. "Just keep bein' yourself."

The conversation was quickly forgotten as Claib slowed the carriage on Richmond's bustling Cary Street. Everywhere they looked, construction was under way. These new buildings, Drewry knew, were to replace the once-sturdy structures that had been destroyed during the War. She tried to visualize this lovely cobbled street as it was before cannonball blasts gouged out craters. Instead, the image of Uncle James and the devastation he'd suffered flickered in her mind.

Matilda climbed down from the carriage. "Ready to go inside, Miss Drew?"

"Yes, of course!" Drewry hurried to join her on the plank sidewalk just as Claib came around to help.

His brow furrowed with confusion. "'Tildy, Miss Drew, it's my job to help y'all down from up there."

With a snort and a grunt, Matilda shushed him. "We done just fine on our own, as you can well see. Now git on over to the feed an' grain an' see if them seeds Mr. Chase ordered done come in."

Claib nodded and headed across the street. "I'll be back here to collect y'all in an hour. Don't keep me waitin' now, hear?"

"I do declare," Matilda said, clucking her tongue, "sometimes that man is downright ornery." She tugged at the store's screen door, then stepped aside to let Drewry enter first.

Drewry rooted through the fabric bin and selected several yards of pale blue organza for Sally's party dress. White lace trim, she decided, and a black velvet bow at the collar, would dress the frock up nicely.

It was as she laid her purchases on the counter that Drewry noticed the tall bookshelves that lined the back wall. *I don't believe my good fortune!* she thought, heading for the leather-bound volumes.

Drewry recalled the first novels she'd ever read, *Angelina Luxmore* and *The Life of a Beauty*. When she outgrew her taste for what she later termed "trivial works," she turned her attention to things like *The Vicar of Wakefield*. But Drewry had always most enjoyed the stories that captured her heart, thanks to strong romantic plots.

She hadn't expected to find books for sale in a general store, of all places, and surely not such a fine selection of them! Almost immediately, Drewry spotted a copy of Charlotte M. Yonge's *Amy Herbert*, and beside it, *David Copperfield*. She could almost see herself, sitting between Sam and Sally on the veranda at Magnolia Grange, inhaling multi-floral roses and sipping mint tea as she read to the children from her favorites.

She grabbed a copy of *Tristam Shandy*. That one, she'd read that one alone in her room at night. And just for good measure, she added *Ministering Children* to the growing stack in her arms.

"Did you leave somethin' up there for somebody else, Miss Drew?" Matilda teased as Drewry plopped her treasures onto the counter.

"Yes, I think I did," she said. "Thank you ever so much for inviting me to accompany you to town!" On an impulse, she threw her arms around the housekeeper. "What a lovely, wonderful day this has turned into!"

Matilda quickly peeled Drewry from her. "I'm touched, Miss Drew, but we ain't at home." She cast a wary glance around the store. "Ain't fittin' to put on such a display in public."

But Drewry knew better. Under the disapproving glare of two women standing near the counter, she realized that what wasn't "fitting" was the open display of friendship between a black and a white. "Tish tosh," she said in her best Suzie imitation. "I'll hug whomever I please, wherever I please, whenever I please." With that, she wrapped Matilda in an even tighter embrace.

Two sharp gasps echoed in the aisle behind them, and once the women were gone, Drewry and Matilda looked at each other. "Good riddance," Drewry muttered just before she and the plump housekeeper burst into gales of laughter.

"Miss Drew," Matilda said, her hand on her heaving bosom, "you an' Mistuh Chase be perfect for one another, 'cause you both 'zactly alike—born troublemakers!"

It was one of the nicest compliments anyone ever paid her.

For the first time since leaving Plumtree Orchards, Drewry felt truly wanted, loved, part of a family. Suddenly, she couldn't wait to get back to Magnolia Grange and tell Chase about the books she'd found. She wanted to tell him how she'd stood up to the old biddies, too.

Then she remembered what Chase had told her about being careful, lest her words put his children in danger…

…and hoped neither Claib nor Matilda would repeat what she'd said!

SEVEN

Summer came quickly and quietly to Magnolia Grange. Before Drewry knew it, the dazzling clouds of pink and white dogwood petals had yielded to the green-gold leaves of summer. The magnolias bloomed, their heavy scent enhanced by the drifting perfume of lilacs and roses, all faithfully tended by Claib.

Drewry often taught the children their lessons outdoors, using a blanket and cushions thrown on the lawn for a schoolroom. "They seem so much more attentive when they're out in the fresh air," she told Chase during one of their evening meetings in his library. "Sam can write his full name on his slate now, plus all of the numbers up to ten."

"Is that so?" Chase's dark eyes surveyed Drewry approvingly. "I must say, my dear Miss Sheffield, you make a fine governess."

Drewry was relieved that the dim light from the oil lamp did not reveal the blush that rose to her cheeks.

"Tell me more about what you're teaching my children."

"Well, Sam's favorite piece from McGuffey's *Reader* is the rhyme of Mary and how her lamb followed her to school." She stifled a little laugh. "Now Sam wants to know if he can bring a lamb into our classroom."

Chase's rich laughter rang out, and Drewry felt a catch in her throat. *Oh, how I love that sound!* Quickly, lest he realize that her feelings for him ran deeper than would be seemly, she continued. "And Sally's favorite is the history of General George Washington, by Mr. Weems, especially the incident concerning the cherry tree, when young George told the truth."

"Ah, that explains why Sally greeted me at the door the other day with the words, 'Father, I cannot tell a lie.'"

"Yes. I must say, that story made quite an impression on her."

The pair lapsed into a companionable silence. They sipped black tea and watched the flickering flames of the lanterns on the walls. Drewry did her best to keep her face and hands relaxed to hide the turmoil that raged within her.

Even a young child like Sally knows to tell the truth, yet I continue to live a lie! But how can I confess my deceit now? Chase would turn me out, I'm sure of it. An honorable man like that would not want a liar teaching his children.

Drewry did her best to stifle her fear. The thought of being separated from her young charges tore at her heart with a force that jolted her. During the past ten weeks as their nanny, teacher, and substitute mother, she'd come to love Sally and Sam as if they were her own. She couldn't bear the thought of losing them. And the same was true of their father!

By the warm, golden glow of the lantern, she stole a glance at Chase. He cut a dashing figure in his high leather boots, black trousers, and white shirtwaist. How handsome he looked with his dark hair parted in the middle and swept back over his ears. She thought his heavy mustache made him appear older than his thirty years and wondered what he'd look like without it. Her heart stirred with tenderness.

During these magical moments in the library each evening, Drewry delighted in their growing camaraderie. Chase often regaled her with stories of his misadventures in attempting to grow delicate hothouse plants. She laughed until tears came to her eyes. Sometimes, he shared his experiences as a Confederate officer, experiences which—and Drewry thanked God for this—had not left him a broken man, like Uncle James.

And always, Chase asked about his children.

Since coming to Magnolia Grange, Drewry had slipped into an easy companionship with Chase, as comfortably as she slipped her hands into a pair of well-worn gloves. In fact, she now felt as though she'd known him forever, and—yes, she could admit her feelings in the privacy of her own heart—had always loved him.

And therein lay the insurmountable problem. She might have hoped he'd grow to love her, too. But how could he, when he didn't know the real Drewry? She tightened her grip around her mug of tea and tried to draw a little comfort from its warmth. The burden of deception grew heavier with each passing day.

Despite the balmy summer evening, Drewry shuddered to recall the anger that had darkened Chase's face when Sheriff Kelly and his band of white-sheeted marauders confronted him that fateful night. "Cowards!" he'd called them. "Children of the Devil, the Fathers of Lies!"

The memory of Chase's searing words branded her heart. *I'm hardly any better than they are!* she anguished. *I'm a coward and a liar to continue this charade. But what else am I to do?*

She watched Chase stare into the lantern's flame. He rubbed his hand over his strong jaw, then pushed back a lock of thick, black hair. She was struck anew with his dark good looks—the sensual mouth; the straight, well-formed nose; the strong chin. But it was those ebony eyes that melted Drewry's heart. Whenever his gaze settled upon her, those eyes seemed to caress her very soul.

She closed her own eyes, feeling utterly miserable and ashamed at having taken advantage of this honorable man's trust. Then she lifted her chin almost imperceptibly and made a silent resolution: *I can't and I won't tell you the truth, Chase Auburn, because I can't bear to lose you.*

⌒

"How many times do I have to tell you, Bridget, that it's not a sin to read the Scriptures?"

Chase picked up the large, leather-bound Bible and opened it for the household's morning devotions. Across the wooden kitchen table, Bridget began to weep. Quickly, Drewry passed her a lace-edged hanky while Matilda, Simon, Claib, and the two children looked on sympathetically.

"Oh, Mister Chase, sir," Bridget said, her thin voice wavering, "back in the old country, my grandma taught me that readin' the Holy Scriptures is a sin and a crime. That kind of learnin' is only for the educated clergy. Sir, I don't want to go to hell." She sniffled loudly into Drewry's hanky.

"Come, come, Bridget," Chase went on. "Why would God have given us His Word if He hadn't wanted us to read it? No disrespect intended, but I fear your dear grandmother was just a little bit mistaken."

At his remark, Bridget burst into a torrent of fresh tears.

Drewry scooted along the wooden bench, put her arm around the girl's heaving shoulders, and smoothed back the wild red locks. "Mr. Chase is right, Bridget," she said, her voice as soothing as if she were comforting one of the children after a nightmare. "Reading the Scriptures is pleasing to God."

Bridget stopped crying and regarded Drewry with red-rimmed blue eyes. "How do ya know that, ma'am?"

"The Lord Jesus Himself told us that '*man shall not live by bread alone, but by every word that proceedeth out of the mouth of*

God,'" said Drewry. "You see, going to church on Sunday and hearing about Jesus is one way of growing closer to the Lord. But reading His Word for ourselves is another."

"Then…'tis really not a sin?"

"Not at all," Chase said. He sent Bridget a kind and understanding smile. "It's a virtue."

For a long moment, everyone waited as Bridget considered this new idea. She took a deep breath, relieved, it seemed. "Well, if that's what the Lord says…" She sniffled one last time, dried her eyes, and stuffed the handkerchief into the pocket of her apron. "Thank you, Miss Drewry. I'll launder your hanky before I return it." She blinked and smiled. "You're a good friend to me, m'lady."

Drewry giggled. "M'lady, indeed!" She squeezed Bridget's hand and said, "You're a good friend, too, dear girl."

"All right, then," said Chase. "Let's begin our devotions, shall we? Would you do us the honor of reading today's psalm, Drewry?"

Watching Drewry read made it difficult for Chase to listen to the Word, because despite the plain shirtwaist and plaid skirt, she *did* look like a proper lady. His very own Lady Nanny.…

"'*Behold, thou desirest truth in the inward parts,*'" Drewry read, pronouncing each word with care, "'*and in the hidden part thou shalt make me to know wisdom.*'"

Even her soft, feminine voice was ladylike, Chase thought. Obviously, Drewry had been trained in the art of elocution. More and more, Chase found himself pondering her upbringing. She'd revealed so little about her past that he couldn't help but wonder if she had a secret to hide. If so, what could be so terrible that she couldn't trust their growing friendship enough to share it with him? "'*Truth in the inward parts.*'" Yes, he desired greatly to know the truth about Drewry Sheffield.

Chase shifted uncomfortably on the wooden bench, drawing a disapproving glance from Matilda, who, since he was a boy, had insisted on stillness and respectful silence during devotions. Chase frowned to himself, because he could not focus on the words Drewry was reading while wondering *why* she could not share her secret with him? She'd proven herself more than competent as a nanny and teacher. That should be sufficient. So why, then, this irresistible urge to know about her past life?

Chase shifted his weight again. He stuffed both hands into his jacket pockets in the hope of stilling his hands, at least. When his fingers brushed the ferrotype of Theresa, a sense of shame immediately flooded over him. How could he dishonor the memory of his beloved wife, mother of his children, by entertaining thoughts of another woman?

Bitter accusations echoed in his head like broken shutters, flapping in a storm. He couldn't quiet them. At length, he buried his head in his hands and let out a groan, and Drewry stopped reading.

"My brothers and sisters, let us pray silently," Chase said in a husky voice, never raising his head. "Please pray for me, that the Lord will create in me a clean heart and renew a right spirit within me."

⌒

Freeland, Maryland
April 10, 1868

My dearest Miss Drew,

Please forgive me for not writing sooner. I didn't get your letter until yesterday. Oh, Miss Drewry, your Uncle James just about went clear out of his head when he found out you was gone. He got drunker than a skunk and tore this place up something terrible.

Why, he even took that cane of his and smashed the mirror atop your dresser, the one that belonged to your great-great-grandmammy! There were glass everywhere, and my Missy done cut her hand real bad trying to clean it up.

And that ain't the half of it. Mr. James took his musket and started waving it at me in the kitchen, real wild like. I throwed up my hands and told him I don't know where you has gone. He say he don't believe me. He wave that musket some more and say he gonna kill me, so I run out the back door to save my skin. He out of his mind, I think!

I stayed in town for a month, and Missy come to see me when she could. She said Porter Hopkins come looking for you that first day after you gone. He say Mr. James going to pay for pulling a fast one on him. Mr. James say, "Don't worry, Hopkins, you is going to get what you got coming."

Oh, Miss Drewry, don't you even think about coming back to this valley of sorrows. Most the hired hands have left, on account of never being paid. Only Missy and me left, 'cause where else would we go?

I am glad you is happy, Miss Drew, and have found yourself a safe place to live, cause this place here ain't no home no more, though me and Missy keep things running as best we can.

Pray for your uncle, Miss Drewry. Ain't nothing going to be right here at Plumtree Orchards until that man get his heart right with the Lord. He needs to trade in that heavy yoke for the light yoke of Jesus.

We be praying for you every day, and know that you is praying for us, too.

Your friend,
Jeb

Drewry sighed heavily as she lit the two lanterns in her bedroom, but not even the iridescence of their flickering glow could lift her spirits.

Grabbing her Bible from the nightstand, she threw herself onto the overstuffed damask chair near the French doors. Outside, the night was black and deep. She lacked the energy even to close the creamy white draperies.

All day long, she had avoided Chase. His strange outburst at their morning devotions continued to haunt her. She longed to reach out to him, to ease whatever was hurting him so badly, but that wasn't possible. She couldn't ask another human being to open his heart to her without responding in kind. She could not listen to his confidences—if, indeed, he would trust her with them—and continue to deceive him. So, she steered clear of him, and for the first time since coming to Magnolia Grange, she excused herself early from their evening chat.

You're a coward and a liar, Drewry Sheffield! Miserably, she sank into the comforting embrace of the soft chair and opened her Bible to the morning's psalm—the Fifty-first—and found the verse that struck her so deeply: *"Behold, thou desirest truth in the inward parts."*

God desires truth. That was not a new concept. But lately, she had organized her life around *hiding* the truth. Oh, how had she gotten herself into this dilemma! Unable to read further, she flipped forward a few pages, and her eyes fell on the sixth verse of Psalm 55: *"Oh that I had wings like a dove! for then would I fly away, and be at rest."*

Yes! To be able to fly away. How she would like to do just that. But deep in her heart, she knew fleeing was not the answer. Where would she go? What would the children do without her? And what would she do without them, without the hope, however remote, of someday becoming more than Chase Auburn's nanny. The very idea stunned her!

Unable to concentrate on her reading, Drewry shut the Bible, closed her eyes, and tried to pray. But, try as she might, her thoughts rambled and scattered in a thousand directions. She wanted to ask God for help, to beg Him to bring some good of the chaos she had made of her life...and brought into Chase's. But she didn't believe He was listening—or that He cared—about her self-made problems. How small and petty they must seem to Him who created all things!

All her pleadings for Uncle James had gone unanswered. Now, her plight seemed worse than ever. Yes, God had deserted her. How could she trust Him when He seemed so far away and silent?

Drewry must have dozed off, for when she was startled into wakefulness, her neck cramped painfully. The room was filled with an unnaturally bright orange light, and she heard a crackling noise coming from outside.

What was that smell? Smoke?

Her Bible fell onto the carpeted floor with a dull thud as she ran to the window. A small scream escaped her throat:

"Fire! The world was on fire!"

EIGHT

Drewry couldn't believe her eyes.

She stood for one terrifying moment, unable to do more than gape at the horror before her. Then she threw open the French doors and rushed out onto the balcony. Heart pounding, she clasped the throat of her high-necked nightdress and stared helplessly at the raging flames. They burned so hot and bright that Drewry could see, despite the lateness of the hour, the sooty gray smoke that roiled above the fiery field.

The world really is on fire!

The entire horizon gave off a red hue, filling the air near the house with thick clouds of smoke, though the fire was several dozen acres away. She hoped against hope that it wasn't Chase's experimental field....

The children...she must go to the children!

Drewry turned to move back inside, intending to be sure the children were still sleeping peacefully, when she caught sight of Chase, sitting low in the saddle of his big black stallion, galloping full-out toward the blaze. *What can he be thinking!* She gripped the white picket railing that enclosed her balcony. *If he rides into that inferno…*

The thought was simply too horrible to contemplate. "Chase!" she shouted, leaning as far over as the rail would allow. "Chase, come back!"

Too late. Already, he was nearly out of sight along the winding path that led from the hired hands' quarters to the outbuildings, then to the pastures and fields beyond the barn. Drewry couldn't tear her eyes from his form, silhouetted against the fire's shimmering brilliance.

Surely he didn't plan to tackle a blaze of such size and magnitude single-handedly! Why, even with the assistance of every hired man on the plantation, the field was as good as gone. Although Drewry had never experienced such a fire before, even she could recognize the truth of that.

She remembered when Matilda and Claib told her how grief-stricken Chase had been after Theresa's death. And that he came to grips with his anguish only after throwing himself into his plant experiments, facing head-on the obstacles of testing new crops in tobacco-tired soil. He was a man of strength and endurance, to be sure, but even Chase had his limits.

Dozens of times, she'd witnessed him in his library—a studious frown lining his handsome brow and a determined gleam in his dark eyes—as he pored over the heavy volumes that lay open on his desk. He'd spared nothing—not time, nor effort, nor money—in setting his plan into motion. But what if this fire cost him everything he'd worked so hard to achieve?

Drewry shuddered involuntarily, thinking of the anguish he must be experiencing as he rode closer and closer to the angry fire's destruction. She was overcome with the need to be with him, to comfort him when he faced the ugly fact that a whole year's work had, quite literally, gone up in smoke.

She ran to her chiffonier and threw open the doors. Grabbing the nearest frock, she slipped out of her nightgown and into the simple, blue cotton dress. She'd barely secured her long, flowing hair with a scrap of ribbon when she heard a soft knock on her door.

"Doo-ree," called a small voice from the hall, "what's that smell?"

"Is it a fire, Drewry?" Sally's tone was edged with anxiety. "Drewry...are you awake?"

Immediately, Drewry opened her door and wrapped both children in a hug. "Yes, children," she began, trying to sound calm and reassuring though her heart hammered inside her, "it's a fire."

She was terrified for Chase—not only because of the physical danger he was facing, but because he was emotionally vulnerable, too. But she hid her concern. The children needed to hear some semblance of the truth, of course, or their fears would only escalate, but she must be brave...for all of their sakes.

"One of the north fields is burning," she explained.

"Where Papa does his sperryments?" Sam asked.

Drewry shrugged. "Possibly."

"Where is he now?" Sally wanted to know.

Drewry sighed. And how was she to answer the child? By telling her that her father had ridden straight into the raging inferno?

She swallowed hard and took a deep breath. Then holding the children at arm's length, she looked them in the eye. "Your father has gone to see if he can put out the fire."

Sam began to cry, and buried his face in Drewry's neck. "He could get burnt up!" he sobbed.

"Hush, now, sweet Sam," she soothed, kissing his soft, round cheek. "Your papa is a brave man. A smart one, too. He won't do anything foolish. I'm sure of it."

She didn't like telling this half-truth. Not one bit. It was precisely becauseshe knew how important the experiments had been to Chase that Drewry's heart continued to thunder. He'd told her as recently as last week that he had invested most of the year's surplus profits in what had, until moments before, thrived in that now-blazing field.

"Will you go to him, Drewry?" Sally asked. "Will you tell him to come back to the house, where he'll be safe?" The little girl blinked, sending a trail of tears down her rosy cheeks.

Using her thumb, Drewry gently wiped them away. "Yes, children, I'll go," she said softly. "But before I do, you must make me a promise."

Sam and Sally exchanged puzzled glances, then focused on their nanny. "What promise, Drewry?" asked Sally. "We'll do whatever you say."

And they would. Not once in her months at Magnolia Grange had the children deliberately disobeyed Drewry, nor given her cause to scold or punish them. Unlike the "spoiled, bratty offspring of a rich man" that Suzie had described on the Richmond-bound train, Sally and Sam were good, sweet-tempered, well-behaved children who tried diligently to please.

"I want you to promise you'll stay inside with Matilda," she cautioned them. "You're not to go out—not for any reason—until I return." Gently, she placed a hand on each child's cheek. "Do you understand?"

Sam and Sally nodded solemnly.

At that moment, Drewry would have done anything humanly possible to say what they wanted to hear—that their father was safe and would be with them soon—but she knew better than to give them false hope. Instead, she forced a faint smile.

"What about the water, Drewry?" asked Sally, her eyes round with wonder. "Is there enough water to put out such a big fire?"

Drewry's forefinger, laid over the girl's quivering lips, silenced her. "I don't know, but your father will think of something...."

Lord, Drewry begged, *guide me. Help me find the words to comfort them.*

It came to her then: "Let's pray, children," she said, pulling them into her arms and speaking the plea that was in her heart.

"Miss Drew, Miss Drew," came an anxious voice, "jus' where do you thinks you is goin'?"

Looking up, Drewry saw Matilda standing in the doorway. "I'm going to look for Chase."

Matilda closed her eyes and folded her hands. "Lawd, Lawd," she prayed aloud, "watch over these bull-headed young'uns of yours. Keep Mr. Chase an' Miss Drew safe."

When Matilda opened her eyes, she also opened her arms, and Sally and Sam leapt from Drewry's bed and ran into her grand-motherly embrace. Looking over their shoulders, Matilda said to Drewry, "Well, get on out of here, then, if you really got a mind to. An' when you find that stubborn man, you tell him this for me: If one hair on his head be singed, I gonna whoop his britches, just like I done when he was a boy."

Nodding, Drewry finished lacing her boots, then slipped past the three, huddled in a teary hug in the hallway, and headed down the stairs.

"And tell him we love him," called Sally as Drewry closed the front door behind her.

～

At the barn, Drewry was surprised to see Claib leading a saddled horse from the building. "Claib! Just where do you think you're going?"

"Why, goin' to see if I can help Mr. Chase."

Drewry frowned. "You'll do no such thing. If something should happen to him, who'd run Magnolia Grange? You're the only one who knows how he'd want things done."

"Ain't nothin' gonna happen to Mr. Chase," Claib said stub-bornly. He stuck his booted foot into the stirrup and prepared to swing astride the bay.

"I hope and pray you're right," Drewry said, pulling his foot out of the stirrup. "But what if the unthinkable *does* happen? Who'll watch over Matilda and Bridget? And what about all the hands and their families, and Sally and Sam? No," she insisted, "he would want you to stay here, where you're needed."

Claib stared across the wide expanse of lawn, mesmerized by the fiery horizon. "I s'pose you're right, Miss Drew. But I can't let you go out there alone. Let me get one of the field hands to go with you."

Drewry shook off his protest. "I'm sure the others are out there already, Claib. And I'm just as sure that not a one of them will be able to talk Chase into coming back here until that fire is under control. Maybe by the time I get there, the good Lord will have put the right words into my mouth, to talk sense into him."

Before the grizzled old man could dissuade her, Drewry climbed into the saddle, slapped the horse's rump, and headed at a full gallop for the burning field.

"You be careful now, Miss Drew!" Claib yelled after her. "Them young'uns loves you like a mama. They don't need to be losin' you, too."

Dry and crackling, bright and blinding, the night air grew hotter as Drewry neared the field. Claib was right. The children did love and need her. *Almost as much as I love and need them. Lord*, she prayed, *keep us all safe.... Use me to bless those little ones at home....*

Even from this distance, Drewry could see that Chase's men had met him at the burning field. No doubt they saw the blaze reflected in the night sky and came to his aid, for there wouldn't have been time to summon them all.

Seeing that this was a field of corn that was aflame and not Chase's experimental field, Drewry breathed a quick prayer of thanksgiving. Still, she had to move quickly. Already, the intensity of the flames was scorching her skin and clothing. Squinting against the brightness, she used the sleeve of her dress to wipe stinging tears from her eyes.

The men, she could see, had tried to protect themselves against the fire by wrapping their faces in wet neckerchiefs. Furiously, some chopped and hacked around the perimeter of the cornfield, while others raked and hoed, creating a fire break that would keep the flames from spreading to adjacent acreage.

But it was a windy night, and tiny golden sparks escaped the parent fire. Like unruly children, they rode the summer breeze, settling on a nearby field. Chase's experimental soy crop!

Helpless, Drewry sat in the saddle, hovering near the tree line, coughing and straining to see through the smoky haze. She wanted to help. But what could she do? Would Chase consider her only a bothersome intrusion?

While she was lost in that moment of indecision, the flurry of activity moved south as Chase and his men tried to head off the fire. Weeks ago, to fight the persistent drought that threatened his experiment, Chase instructed the men to lay mounds of field grass over the soil to protect the delicate roots from the harsh, drying effects of the blazing summer sun.

The thatch had saved the plants.

Now, it could very well mean the end of them.

Dry and parched, the clippings were fuel for the ravenous flames. With a sinking sensation, Drewry knew that the most they could hope for was to keep the fires in these two fields from spreading and destroying any more of Magnolia Grange. *I can't sit idly by a moment longer!* she decided. *I'm going to do what I can!*

Tying her horse to a tree downwind an acre or two from the fire, Drewry hitched up her skirts and ran toward the field. When she got there, she spied a mattock on the ground. Grabbing it, she fell into line alongside Chase's men. Hoisting the heavy tool, she began methodically chopping at the hard, encrusted earth that ringed the fire.

"Miss Sheffield!" Chase thundered when he noticed her. "What are you doing out here? And who's minding my children?"

With the back of her hand, Drewry wiped beads of perspiration from her brow and squinted through the thick, roiling smoke. "Matilda, of course," she retorted, stomping over to where he stood, pickax in hand. Not once in the months Drewry had been at Magnolia Grange had she seen Chase so angry. Or was it grief that creased that handsome brow?

"Chase," she began, her tone gentler now, "it hasn't rained in weeks, and these fields are as dry as straw. This is a wildfire. Even I know that. Send the men back to their cottages—they've done all they can—and come back to the house with me, where it's safe."

His broad shoulders slumped, as if bowed beneath a great burden, as he looked out across the burning fields.

She took a step closer, and forced him to meet her gaze. "Chase Auburn, you listen to me!" Drewry gestured toward the men, working feverishly to keep the fire at bay. "Someone could be seriously injured. Someone could die." She paused, then continued, "Are these fields worth risking even one life?"

For an instant, he met her eyes, and in that instant, Drewry saw an aching sadness. She started to reach out, to touch him, but he sagged to his knees.

"Gone," he rasped. "All gone. A year of hard work, three years of study before that, gone."

He seemed lost in thought. Looking down at him, Drewry was reminded of her own helplessness when attempting to console her Uncle James. *Lord*, she prayed, *speak through me. Give Chase, your servant, peace. Ease his burden....*

Tentatively, she placed a hand on his shoulder. She longed to say something—anything—to reassure him. But nothing came. No comforting words. No direction. Nothing.

Chase did not even look up. "Go back to the house, Drewry." His tired voice was laced with bitterness. "Go away. Go away and leave me alone. Please."

Her own eyes burned with tears—as much from sadness and rejection as from the smoke and soot. There were tears in his eyes, too. Because of the fire…yet another loss…or was it something more?

He's ashamed that I've seen him like this, she decided. Drewry couldn't leave him—not now.

With sudden inspiration, she dropped to her knees beside him. "Oh, Chase," she cried, "I'm so afraid! I can't go back to the house in this state…. I—I'll frighten the children." She held her breath. It was true, after all. She *was* frightened—for Chase's well-being more than anything else.

"Won't you pray with me, Chase?" What could it hurt? Even with no answer to her last desperate plea, she somehow believed that God was watching over Chase, and would answer on his behalf. Without waiting for a reply from Chase, she began asking the Lord for His mercy, for strength to endure whatever came next….

But Chase did not close his eyes, nor did he turn his face toward heaven, as Drewry instinctively had. Instead, he kept his gaze focused on her—hands folded piously, eyes closed in concentration.

Then, suddenly, as if in answer to her prayer, the skies opened up and a hard steady rain began to fall. Wonderingly, Chase held out his hands, palm up, and watched as the droplets rolled from his fingertips. The soothing sound of Drewry's prayer blended with the pattering of raindrops on the wide brim of his black felt hat. And mercifully, as she prayed, with every drop of the heavenly liquid, the fields burned with less fury.

He glanced at Drewry in amazement. Her face, illuminated by the fire's fading glow, appeared angelic to him as she knelt there beside him, so lost in prayer that it seemed she was oblivious to the smoldering all around her.

When she concluded her prayer at last, Chase lifted her chin with the tip of his forefinger and stared deep into her eyes. Then, ever so lightly, he kissed her cheek. "Thank you, Drewry, for reminding me that all is not lost. Go back to the house now. I'll be along shortly."

He rose, drawing her to her feet, but she made no move to leave. "If you're staying, I'm staying," she declared, "because...well, because you're a—a friend, that's why, and what are friends for, if not to be there for one another in times of trouble?"

Chase sighed deeply, staring across his destroyed fields.

Then, shaking his head, he smiled in resignation. "You are a true friend indeed, Drewry Sheffield, and I wouldn't be surprised if you weren't a messenger of the Lord, too."

If you only knew, she thought, *that I'd like to be more, so much more than a friend, Chase Auburn....*

Such an admission could never be confessed, she knew, not to such a fine and honorable man, whose love for his wife still burned as brightly as the fire that had ravaged these fields only a short while ago. Besides, he deserved better than the likes of Drewry Sheffield, who had lived a lie all these many months.

Putting hope behind her, she squared her shoulders. *Well, you may never be his wife, but he has said you are his friend. You'll just have to be satisfied with that.* "Let's go back to the house now, Chase. The children are worried about you...."

Chase took a last lingering look at the smoldering field before turning his back on it. As they slowly walked side by side, he said, "Why did you come out here tonight? Why didn't Claib come, instead?"

"He was ready to leave, but I talked him out of it."

Chase frowned. "Claib loves this place every bit as much as I do, and worked on those fields almost as hard as I did. I can't imagine what you could have said to keep him away."

Drewry shrugged. "I simply pointed out that if something happened to you, you'd want him to run Magnolia Grange, until you were back on your feet, of course."

"Ahhh, of course," he said, understanding registering in his deep voice. "But why did you come, Drewry? Why didn't you send Simon to bring back the news that I was safe?"

Because I had to see for myself, she wanted to say. Instead, she explained, "Because we—that is, the children and Matilda and… and everyone—were very worried about you."

A tired smile lifted the corners of his mouth. "But weren't you afraid…of the fire?"

Without a moment's hesitation, she said, "I was far more afraid of losing you."

He stopped in his tracks and, despite the pelting rain, stared into her face. Basking in the warmth of his gaze, Drewry's heart raced.

Suddenly, his smile faded, and he brought a damp and sooty wad of paper from his shirt pocket. "I found this tacked to a tree just outside the fire line," he told her, indicating the still smoldering fields with a jerk of his head. "If you're to help me tell Matilda and the children the truth, you'll need to know all the facts."

Frowning, Drewry took the note from him and smoothed it out before reading aloud the words scribbled in haste: "'We warned you not to act like a Yankee! Next time we'll ruin something a lot more valuable than one of your sorry little crop experiments.'"

Her heart was pounding now—with full-blown dread. She looked from Chase's scowling face to the scrap of paper still clutched in her hand. "Oh, Chase, it's the Klan again, isn't it?"

"Yes," he hissed, relieving her of the threatening message and jamming it deep into his jacket pocket. "Alden Kelly and his merry band of misfits."

Drewry covered her face with both hands. "It's all my fault. If I had just minded my own business that day when he came by…."

Unexpectedly, Chase tugged her hands away from her face and stroked her rain-soaked hair. "They didn't do this because of anything you did or said, Drewry," he assured her. "They did it because, despite their repeated threats, I refuse to allow them to intimidate me."

There in the protective circle of his arms, she felt the warmth that radiated from his powerful body. But she also felt his muscles, tensed with concern and anxiety. "They've threatened you before?" she whispered.

Chase nodded. "Nothing as blatant as their midnight visit...." He glanced toward the fields. Smoke still billowed above the glow of embers now coating the once-green earth. "Or this..." He patted the pocket that held the note.

He shook his head sadly. "It's been small things mostly. Snide remarks in town. Dirty looks." He chuckled. "Suddenly I was an outcast when, until recently, my name was clearly part of Richmond's social register."

Their faces were mere inches apart when she looked up at him. "What will we tell the children?"

"We'll just say that the men in white robes didn't like what I was growing out there. We'll tell everyone to be careful, to stay close to the house, to—"

"But wouldn't it be better to pretend it was an accident..." she broke in, "...to keep them from worrying unnecessarily?"

His brow furrowed and he backed away. "I'm surprised at you, Miss Sheffield. I thought you and I were of one mind when it came to dealing with the truth."

The edge in his voice was chilling.

Drewry remembered their brief conversation that night, alone in the kitchen, after the Klan had paid its frightening midnight visit. Drewry sighed. When she disembarked from the train in Richmond and allowed Chase to think she was the nanny he'd

sent for, she promised herself there would be no further decep-
tions. *But you're becoming so proficient at lying, it seems the natural
thing to do!*

"Of course," she said quietly. "What was I thinking? The truth
is always best."

"It's not going to be easy, telling them what happened, of
course." Chase took a step nearer and gazed down into her eyes
once more. "But it will be easier…if you'll be there beside me."

"Oh, Chase, you know I'll be there, always!" Before she could
think what she was doing, she lifted her face, stood on tiptoe, and
pressed her lips against his. She kissed him long and hard. To dis-
tract him? To comfort him? She didn't know. Nor did she care.
She only knew that it felt good and right to be in his arms. To feel
his sweet, rain-wet lips on hers.

It ended all too soon. "Oh, my. I—I'm so sorry!" she stam-
mered, putting her back to him. "I don't know what came over me.
I only meant to…" Drewry heaved a sigh of frustration. "I don't
know what I meant to do!"

Chase pulled her back into his embrace and placed a fingertip
over her lips. "Shhh," he whispered. "It's all right. It's been a very
long and difficult night for both of us. You only meant to console
me."

Then, taking her hand to lead her through the rutted field,
they began walking toward the tree where she'd tethered the horse.
The animal plodded quietly along behind them as they walked in
silence, across the damp lawn, into the barn. And once the beast
was safe inside its stall, they walked around the circular flowerbed
near the drive, up the brick steps, and across the marble-floored
foyer.

They paused just outside the kitchen, where a light gleamed
from beneath the door. Soft voices floated to them…Matilda and
Sam and Sally.

"Before we go in there," he said, "I want you to know that I think you're a remarkable woman." Then he gave her hand a little squeeze, and thrust open the swinging doors.

"How about a cup of warm milk and some of Matilda's good cookies?" he called cheerfully as he burst into the room. Then, kissing each of his children soundly, Chase added, "Since you're all up anyway, we might as well make a party of it!"

For the moment, the children forgot their fears and giggled at his antics. Over the heads of the children, Matilda and Claib exchanged puzzled glances. Just what was Mistuh Chase up to?

The truth would be told soon enough, his level look conveyed; for now, at least, they would celebrate.

Drewry stood alone, one hand pressed to each swinging door, peering into the kitchen. *You're a remarkable woman*, he'd said. Her heart swelled with the love she felt for him.

But almost immediately, her elation drained away, like the air in a child's balloon. Chase had walked away from her kiss as easily as he'd shaken rain from his hat. And reacted to her offer of friendship with kindly deference, not passion. Now she was mortified at the thought of her impetuous gesture....

Yes, she loved him, and Drewry supposed it was good that this rude awakening had happened tonight, while her love was fresh and new, rather than months from now, when it would no doubt burn deep in her heart.

The most she could ever hope for was to be his friend...and to love him from afar.

NINE

*D*ear Jeb,

There's so much to tell you, I hardly know where to begin. I have lost many nights' sleep, worrying about you and the others at Plumtree Orchards. I know how difficult Uncle James can be even under the best of circumstances. My running off and leaving him alone to deal with Porter Hopkins didn't improve his disposition, I'm sure. I'm so sorry that my cowardice has put all of you at risk. I can only hope that someday you'll forgive me.

This lie I'm living steals my rest, and I must confess that guilt is at the root of those lost hours' sleep, as well. I can't tell you how many times I've wanted to confess my sin to Chase. On the one hand, because he's a good-hearted, honest man, he may appreciate my "confession." On the other, because he's so decent and honorable, he may despise me for having deceived him at all.

What am I to do, Jeb? Oh, how I miss having you near to advise me. I suppose this misery is my penance for living as I have these past months.

*Please don't worry about me, though. For all my whimpering,
I am truly happy here at Magnolia Grange. It's the weight of the
lie that gets me down from time to time, that's all.*

*Give Missy a hug for me, and be sure to tell everyone that I
send my best and my blessings. Tell them they're in my thoughts
and prayers each and every day, and that I miss them all very
much!*

Of course, I miss you most of all, dear Jeb.

With my deepest affection,
Drewry

Thanks to the blanket of hay that had been strewn to protect the soy crop from the drought, Drewry soon learned, Chase's
experimental field had not been totally destroyed after all. The
soybeans proved to be hardy plants, and very few were devoured
by the ravenous flames.

All too soon, however, the clippings caused a problem of an
entirely different sort. As the thatch lay heaped upon the ground,
it absorbed the rain like a sponge. And as the days passed and the
moisture between the thin blades multiplied, rot set in.

Squatting between the tidy rows, Chase held his hat in one
hand and overturned the leaves of one plant with the other.
"Fungus!" he spat out. "We have ourselves a raging, spreading
fungus here, every bit as damaging as that fire would have been."

Claib knelt beside his boss and inspected the plant. "What we
gonna do now?"

Chase shook his head glumly. "We're going to get rid of the
thatch, for starters, and then we're going to pinch off the affected
leaves. It'll be time consuming, painstaking work, but it has to be
done." Sighing, he rose, shoved his hands into his pockets, and stared
at the toes of his dusty boots. "And if it doesn't work, we'll wash and
dry the fungus from every single leaf by hand, if we have to!"

"How we gonna make time to do that?" Claib wanted to know. "We got to get set to bring in the other crops."

Chase frowned. "Where's your faith, man! There's time enough…if we don't waste any more of it whimpering!"

Claib clenched his weathered hat in his hands. "We only got just so much time and so many hired hands." He glanced at the field of struggling soy plants and shook his head.

Chase flexed a muscle in his jaw as he replaced his wide-brimmed black felt hat and turned to face his foreman. "It'll get done. We'll *see* that it does. If we have to work all day, every day, and if we have to light this field with lanterns to see what we're doing at night, we'll do it!"

It was Claib's turn to sigh. "If you say so, Mr. Chase." The older man shuffled off toward the barn, muttering under his breath. "Don't see how he plans to save this field and harvest all the rest, though." Claib pulled his hat low on his forehead as he disappeared into the barn.

Chase ignored Claib's negative remarks. *The experiment was working!* he reminded himself. He'd been a gnat's breath away from proving he could make a success of this newfangled plant called the soybean. *If it hadn't been for the Klan's intervention…*

But he would not allow those lunatic vigilantes to stop him. He'd post guards at all four corners of Magnolia Grange, if need be, and arm them with shotguns to protect against another Klan attack.

Drewry's words echoed in his mind: *Is it that important?*

He sighed deeply. The experiment was important, but certainly not worth a man's life…not even the life of a Klansman.

Dejected, Chase slumped against the fence that surrounded the barnyard. Chickens clucked around his feet, pecking contentedly at the seeds Matilda had scattered earlier that morning. He was tired. Too tired, even, to shoo them away when they tapped at the toes of his boots. He'd felt much the same weariness the night before, when, on hands and knees, he tried in vain to smother the billowing flames with nothing more than an old horse blanket.

"Chase?"

Drewry's voice, like a gentle breeze, reached him. *It's as if she can read my moods,* Chase thought, looking over his shoulder to find the young woman, dressed in a pink frock, heading his way. She looked lovely with her dark hair falling free around her shoulders that way. She'd tied the top part up, he noticed, with a ribbon the same shade of pink as her dress.

In spite of his somber mood, Chase smiled. "What brings you out here so early in the day?"

"I was chatting with Matilda in the kitchen and saw you out here alone." She fumbled to find the pockets in her dress. "I—I just wondered if there was anything wrong."

Oh, but she was a vision, standing there looking up into his face with those big, dark, luminous eyes of hers. Though she was close enough to touch, he dared not, for fear he'd succumb to the same schoolboyish behavior he allowed himself to display last night. She'd only meant to offer him comfort, and he'd taken full advantage of it.

"Can I get you anything?" she asked. "A glass of lemonade, a cup of tea?"

"No. Nothing, thank you. I'm about to ride out to the north fields." He glanced toward the back porch, where Matilda was shaking dust from the kitchen doormat. "So tell me, what exciting lessons have you planned for the children today?"

"I thought after they finished their lessons, we'd take a walk and—"

"And I thought I made it clear that everyone is to stay close to the house," he snapped. Immediately, he regretted his harsh tone, for her fresh-faced enthusiasm wilted like a flower in the sun. "I'm sorry," he said with a sigh. "It's just that I'm concerned for your safety. Yours, and the children's, of course."

"I'd only intended to take them as far as the pond," she explained, her eyes downcast. "I thought perhaps we could catch tadpoles, so the children could study how they become frogs."

Chase chuckled in relief. "Of course. How silly of me not to trust you. I should know by now that you have my children's best interests at heart."

He wanted to say more, so much more. He wanted to tell her how lovely she looked in her plain pink dress. He wanted to tell her how ridiculous he felt for jumping to conclusions. He wanted to tell her she had the biggest, brownest eyes he'd ever seen, and the sweetest, softest lips….

Chase cleared his throat, removed his hat, and slid its brim between thumb and forefinger, round and round. He wanted to tell her how sorry he was for the way he'd behaved last night, when she'd caught him blubbering like a babe, and kissed him. He should never have surrendered to it. *Forgive me, sweet Drewry*, he wanted to say, *for my display of weakness last night*. Instead, Chase closed his eyes. *And forgive me, my darling Theresa, for betraying your memory in the arms of another woman.*

"Well," she said in a small voice, glancing toward the house, "I'll just fetch the children, then, and we'll be on our way to the pond."

First, he'd frightened her with his harsh accusation, Chase thought miserably. And now he'd made her uncomfortable with his hemming and hawing. He would have given anything to start the conversation over again.

"Matilda will protest at first, but I'm sure you can convince her to let you borrow a few canning jars for the project." Chase gave her a wink and, without even thinking, reached out and tenderly touched her cheek.

Drewry's smile widened, he noticed, and the gentle, loving light returned to her eyes.

"She is more bark than bite, isn't she?"

Chase blinked. "Oh...Matilda, you mean," he said distractedly. "Yes. All bark and no bite."

Drewry took a step back, turned, and headed for the kitchen. "Matilda says she's fixing ham and pea soup for lunch," she called to him from the bottom step of the porch. "Perhaps I'll ride out with some when it's ready."

With that, she stepped into the kitchen and quietly closed the screen door behind her.

Chase stood, hand still extended as it had been when he touched her cheek. *She's out of your reach*, he told himself. *Completely out of your reach. And for her sake, that's the way it should stay.*

⌣

Drewry shifted uneasily on the old oak pew. No matter how hard she tried to concentrate, her thoughts kept drifting from the worship service. Her conscience stung as painfully as when she'd pricked her finger on a blackberry bramble.

She peeked at the faces of the people sitting nearby, their heads reverently bowed. Each seemed intent on the minister's prayers of intercession. Drewry smiled, recalling how warmly the good people of Calvary Church had welcomed her as one of their own. Over the summer, she came to know them and looked forward to their conversations at the socials after Sunday school and church.

They accepted her as part of the Auburn family. In fact, Drewry often wondered if several of the ladies of the missionary society hadn't already pegged her for the next Mrs. Auburn. To the casual observer, she supposed that she, Chase, and the children—sitting together in the Auburn pew—did resemble any one of the young families that comprised the congregation of this country church. Yes, she had been accepted without question and without reservation. And therein lay the source of her prickly conscience.

Oh, Lord, I know it's wrong to keep up this deceit, but I'm so far in now, I don't know how to get myself out.

Just as often as Drewry considered confessing her charade to Chase, she changed her mind. These people seemed to love her, but they loved her because they believed her to be something she was not. If they discovered the real Drewry Sheffield, she reasoned, they'd cast her away as easily and heartlessly as Uncle James had.

The services at Calvary—inspiring sermons and enthusiastically sung hymns—reminded Drewry of her church back home in Freeland. The Sheffields, too, had had their own pew, and in those early years, she'd sat between her mama and papa. After their deaths, it was Uncle James who sat beside her. When he stopped attending services, she sat alone. How wonderful it was to be included in a family again, a family she could call her own...until the day when she found the courage to admit her true identity.

She exhaled a trembly sigh, which drew a concerned look from Chase.

"Is everything all right?" he mouthed.

Over the heads of the children, she smiled and nodded, wishing she could tell him the truth. But that was quite out of the question. She couldn't risk being abandoned again. Surely God had not expected such an impossible thing of her.

Did He?

Practically the entire congregation had come to church that morning, Drewry guessed as she glanced again around the crowded sanctuary. Young boys, mimicking the behavior of their farmer fathers, sat stiffly in their Sunday suits, while the women and girls perched on the pews in their best frocks, bedecked with ribbons and lace in a bouquet of summer colors.

The swish of fans filled the humid air. From the corner of her eye, Drewry saw that even Chase was fanning himself with Sally's pink shell-shaped fan. It looked so silly in his big, tanned hands that she struggled to stifle a giggle. Only a man as sure of his manhood as Chase could use a lady's fan without embarrassment, she thought. But then, Chase's confidence was just one of the many things she cherished about him.

Sally passed Drewry one of the paper fans provided by the usher. "You look all red-faced and sweaty, Drewry," she whispered loudly, looking like a cherub in a yellow straw bonnet encircled with a halo of pink roses.

Drewry patted the girl's hand and pretended to listen to every word of Pastor Tillman's sermon. *I'm hot, all right,* she thought angrily. *Hot under the collar of all this Sunday finery! I have a home now. Respect. Affection. And I'll not risk it all just to ease my sorry excuse of a conscience!*

"As faithful Christians," Pastor Tillman was saying, "we do the right thing...not so much because we fear God's punishment, but because this is how we show the world that we are imitating the life of our Lord, Jesus Christ."

Drewry gasped. It was as if the pastor had read her mind! "We must strive to mature as Christians," he continued. "To grow up, not just in body, but in spirit."

She considered his words a moment longer. Then, defiantly, Drewry sat up straighter and squared her shoulders. She folded her white-gloved hands over the fan in her lap and lifted her chin. *If a guilty conscience is the price for my happy life at Magnolia Grange, I'll just have to learn to live with it!*

⌒

Chase closed his eyes and tried in vain to focus on the sermon. Only moments before, Drewry told him with that polite nod of her head that all was well, but he didn't believe her for an instant. He had eyes, after all. He could see that something was definitely wrong. That sigh...it sounded as if the weight of the Confederacy rested on her slender shoulders.

Yes, indeed, Miss Drewry Sheffield, as much as you may deny it, there's something terribly amiss in your life. Just as there's something amiss in mine.

The memory of Drewry's sudden, impassioned kiss flooded his mind. His temples pounded as he recalled her lips, pressed to his, the way her slender body felt against his own.

Her boldness had taken him by surprise, to be sure, yet as his arms instinctively closed around her, kissing her seemed the most natural thing in the world. And wasn't her no-nonsense boldness one of the qualities he admired most about her?

He remembered the raw hurt that glittered in her dark eyes when he pulled away from their embrace and held her at arm's length. He hadn't said a word, but something told him she'd read his silence as blatant rejection.

The conflict that tore at his soul was almost like physical pain. He wanted to gather Drewry to him and declare his undying love, and yet, how could he? He'd promised that kind of love to Theresa. Besides, he didn't dare risk loving like that again. It simply hurt too much when it was gone.

Opening his eyes, he caught Drewry shifting on the hard bench. *How thoughtless of you, Chase Auburn. You should have brought cushions for her and the children. You know Pastor Tillman is not known for the brevity of his sermons.*

He noticed Drewry patting his daughter's hand after accepting one of those contraptions the pastor called fans. He smiled. Already, the children treated her more like a mother than a nanny. How quickly the web of love had woven those three together!

Could he dare allow himself to be part of that silken web? Would she even want him? Her kiss seemed to promise that she would....

Almost unconsciously, Chase's hand sought the ferrotype of his wife, hidden in the pocket of his coat. There was no need to take it out and examine it, for her likeness was etched in his mind.

His lovely Theresa, with her long dark hair, her coal-black eyes, her wistful smile, had died giving him Sam. How could he betray her memory with such thoughts!

Overwhelmed with emotion, Chase closed his eyes again. He remembered his wife the last time he saw her alive, her skin as waxen white as the pillowslip on which she laid. It broke his heart to hear her words then, and they came back to him now with a fresh pang of grief: "You must remarry, Chase," she'd said, her voice thin and labored. "I don't want you and the children to be alone. The Lord will bring you a new love. And when He does, I expect you to accept her as a gift!"

He stared blankly at Drewry, absent-mindedly twining a strand of her dark hair round her finger, and his heartbeat doubled. Right there in the second row of the Calvary Church, during Sunday services no less!

He didn't want a new love. His fingers tightened around the handle of the fan he held, almost snapping the fragile wood in two. Fear and guilt—his two crusty old friends. Far easier to live with these two than to face the unknown territory of new love.

"You is as stubborn a man as I ever knowed," Matilda had chastised earlier that week. "Come in here all down in the dumps, sayin' you don't know why. Hmpf!"

"I'm fine," he defended. "I'm not down in the—"

"Mr. Chase, I been lookin' into them eyes of yours ever since I powdered your li'l round bottom. Don't tell me you is fine, 'cause I know perfectly well that you *ain't*."

Chase knew better than to argue with Matilda. He perched on a high stool and stared sullenly, silently, into the mug of coffee she'd poured him.

"I'll tell you why you look so sorrowful. You is afraid of Miss Drew, that's what!"

His head snapped up at her remark. "Afraid of her! Why, that's rubbish! She's no bigger than a minute."

She wagged a plump finger under his nose. "Now, now, I'm not sayin' you ain't a brave man. You wasn't scared to teach your hired hands to read an' write. You wasn't afraid of provin' you could grow more than tobaccy and cotton out yonder. An' you didn't let folks in town keep you from openin' the first hothouse in these parts. Yet you is afraid to admit how you feel 'bout Miss Drewry." She threw up her hands. "I declare, I don't know what-all I'm gonna do with you!"

He remained silent, both hands wrapped tightly around the big white coffee mug, knowing she hadn't finished her tongue-lashing yet.

"You think Miss T'resa want you to be unhappy? I was there when she died, and don't you forget it. I heard every word she said to you at the end."

Chase took a deep breath. *Where's your courage, man! What if Drewry, even with her secret past, is the woman Theresa prayed God would bring into your life? Who are you to go against the will of God!*

As Pastor Tillman wound up his sermon, Chase kept his eyes closed. Deep within himself, he found that quiet spot of resignation, where he stood before his Creator and admitted that he was not the master of his own fate. Truth was, he hadn't been for many years—not since the day he renewed his commitment to Christ as a young man in this very church.

He shook his head. *Thy will be done, Lord*, he prayed. *Thy will be done.*

When Chase opened his eyes, he found Drewry studying him. She blushed to her hair roots, he noticed, before quickly turning away.

And yet again, his heart thundered in response.

TEN

Dear Miss Drew,

*I read your letter to Missy, and she say to tell you she loves
you and is praying for you. She says don't worry 'bout us here
at Plumtree Orchards, 'cause your uncle is quieter these days.
Maybe, the good Lord is gonna answer our prayers and set
this man free from his demons, after all.*

*I understand why you feel bad about telling that lie, Miss
Drew. Nobody blames you for telling it, least of all, sweet
Jesus. What could you do but leave this place? Not a one of us
wanted to see you married to old Porter Hopkins!*

*You was brung up to live by God's law, so you ain't used to
telling lies. And that means nothing will make you feel better,
except the truth.*

*Go to Mr. Chase and tell him. If he is as kind and honor-
able as you say, he will understand. Maybe not at first, but
he will remember all the good you been doing for his children,
and the many times you gave him kind words, too. Even if the
truth makes him angry, you got to tell it. "'The truth shall set*

you free,'" say the Good Book. You ain't going to feel free or right with your life again till everything is out in the open.

Sound to me like you love this man, Miss Drew. Missy say to tell you to "build on a strong foundation," like the Bible say. Start on the right foot.

We're praying for you, like always.

Your good friend,
Jeb

Drewry held the letter in her hands and wept, glad she had the foresight to close her door before opening the envelope. She knew Jeb was right. For as long as she could remember, she'd started each day reciting John 13:15: *"For I have given you an example, that ye should do as I have done to you."* For as long as she could remember, she had lived by that Golden Rule…

…until coming to Magnolia Grange.

Drewry replaced Jeb's letter in the envelope and sat back in the morning seat. Christ would not have lied to anyone, not for any reason, the way she'd lied to Chase. He would not have continued the life of deception, as she had. She knew that if she was ever to begin trying to pattern her life after the Lord's, she must tell Chase everything, just as Jeb suggested.

But Drewry wondered if she possessed enough inner strength to tell him the whole truth. She would need mountains of spiritual strength to live with his disapproval…and possible rejection.

She crossed the room and sat at her desk. Grasping the brass drawer pull, she heard the quiet protest of the wood against wood as she eased open the drawer. Withdrawing a sheet of creamy vellum, she placed it on the forest-green desk blotter. The quill's tip clinked quietly against the tiny glass jar as she carefully dipped it into the ink:

Dearest Jeb,

I received your latest letter, and I assure you, I have taken your good advice to heart. It pleases me to hear that Uncle

James has been behaving more like his old self of late. You can be sure that I'll continue praying for his healing!

And I beseech your continued prayers, too, as some very peculiar things have been going on around here. Matilda says the things I've been hearing and smelling are caused by ghosts! She is a spirited old thing and enjoys seeing my stunned reaction to her stories. But, seriously, there is no rational explanation for what has been going on in the middle of the night.

I can't tell you how many times I've stood on my balcony, overlooking the lawn, and caught the scent of a cigar. I've heard muffled voices, too, and, occasionally, what sounds like a man's cough. But it's the sound of wicked laughter that tells me that the Klan has been keeping an eye on us here at Magnolia Grange for quite some time. I fear that burning Chase's experimental field was only the first of many horrible surprises they have in store for us if he doesn't give in to their demands.

I didn't mention the fire to worry you, Jeb, for we are all well. I mention it only because it is the reason I cannot yet tell Chase the truth. So for now, while he has so much on his mind, I'll keep my dreadful secret.

Remember that I think of you often and pray for you always. Give my love to Missy and the others.

Fondly,
Drewry

It's all well and good for Jeb to preach honesty, but he's not nor has ever been in a situation quite like this! Drewry impatiently snapped the pink linen cloth across the long table in preparation for Sally's birthday party.

"What's wrong with you, Miss Drew?" Matilda asked from across the dining room, where she was decorating the sideboard with gaily colored paper streamers and big yellow letters that spelled out "Happy Birthday, Sally."

"It's nothing, Matilda." Drewry smoothed the cloth with her hands, then stepped back to eye the effect. "I'm just tired, I guess."

"You is more than tired. You been like a cat on a hot tin roof these days. I been watchin' you. Somethin' troublin' you, missy, an' I knows it!" She waddled to the kitchen, muttering to herself about secret-keeping, and fetching a tray to carry the party foods.

Drewry busied herself with an arrangement of fresh-picked purple grapes and butter cookies on a three-tiered silver cake stand.

"When we're finished, maybe I'll take a nap with the children," Drewry said nonchalantly. "I'll have plenty of time, since the guests aren't to arrive until 4:30."

In the process of trying to balance a dozen little red sugar-dusted cakes on the top tier, her hand slipped. Before she knew it, the whole thing toppled, sending grapes and cakes cascading down onto petit fours.

Frantically, Drewry reached out to right the stand, but succeeded only in knocking over the cut glass pitcher of lemonade, the contents of which flooded the table and dripped onto the hardwood floor.

"Oh, no! Even Sally's birthday cake has been splashed with lemonade!" Drewry groaned, putting her hands to her face.

Matilda was at her side in an instant. "There, there, honey lamb," she whispered, wrapping Drewry in a massive hug. "You just hush now, and come with me."

Drewry allowed herself to be led to the white wicker settee on the porch.

"Don't you worry none," Matilda soothed, patting her shoulder. "There's plenty more food where that come from. It's you I'm worried 'bout."

The compassionate tone of Matilda's voice, along with her reassuring hug, put a lump in Drewry's throat.

"I think I knows what's botherin' you, Miss Drew."

She couldn't possibly know, Drewry thought. Because if she knew, Matilda couldn't treat her with such kindness.

Matilda pulled an envelope from her apron pocket. "This was with the rest of the mail I collected from the post office last week," she explained, handing it to Drewry. "It's addressed to Mr. Chase, I know, but since it's part of my job to get the household bills ready for him to pay, I always open his mail."

Drewry slid the letter from its official-looking envelope. The moment her eyes fell on the letterhead—"Wheatley Employment Agency, Baltimore, Maryland"—her heart sank. Alarmed, she met Matilda's knowing look.

"These nice people want to know if Mr. Chase be happy with the nanny they sent him…a girl named Suzie something-or-other."

Drewry sighed heavily and nodded. "I was her seatmate all the way to Richmond."

"You gonna tell ole Matilda about it?" The twinkle in her eyes told Drewry she was safe.

Within moments, she'd spilled the whole ugly story.

"Mmmm." Matilda nodded sagely. "You'd best tell Mr. Chase, soon as you can."

Drewry shook her head. "I can't. Not yet."

"Why not, child? You love that man and he loves you. You mark my words: 'The truth shall set you free,'" she quoted.

Drewry groaned quietly. "He won't understand. How could he! He's too good, too decent, too honest…."

"Lay this problem at the feet of Jesus, honey lamb. Whatever ails you, take it to Him."

Drewry pulled away from Matilda's touch. "What's the use in that?" she shot back. "God has never answered my prayers before. Well, hardly ever," she amended, remembering the night of the drought-breaking rain. "When I was an orphan, I begged Him to bring my mama and my papa back. And then, when Uncle James kept getting worse…"

Drewry found herself enclosed in another bear hug. For several moments, Matilda hummed softly, rocking her back and forth as if she were a distraught child. Drewry relaxed into the motherly embrace and found herself comforted. It occurred to her that even though Matilda knew the whole awful truth about her, she loved her still.

The older woman pointed to the cloudless blue sky. "You see them stars, Miss Drewry?"

Drewry couldn't help giggling. "Of course not. It's broad daylight!"

She waited patiently, wondering where Matilda's discourse was leading.

"Sometimes, in the dark o' night, a shootin' star will suddenly come into view, and we may think it just appeared from nowhere. But it was really there all along."

Drewry looked heavenward, at a sky filled with hidden stars.

"Don't you see? It's like you, lookin' for answers to your prayers. God don't always answer with a yes or a no. Sometimes, His answer be *not yet*."

Despite the heat of the day, a chill crept down Drewry's back. *Matilda is absolutely right. Why haven't I realized it before!*

"The answers to your prayers are like them stars," the woman said softly. "Just 'cause you can't see 'em don't mean they ain't there. God is like that, honey pie. He always answers your prayers. Mebbe not like you want Him to, but He always does what He know is best for you."

Drewry smiled into her friend's face. "Thank you, Matilda," she said, "for teaching me to look for hidden stars. I've been behaving like a spoiled little girl all my life, demanding proof that God loves me."

She stood and announced, "I think it's high time for me to behave like a grown-up!"

⁓

A bevy of little girls in party dresses and boys in sailor suits milled about in the front parlor, balancing teacups and plates of finger foods like miniature adults. Some made strained, polite conversation, while others sat quietly, listening to the violin quartet that filled the house with the soft music of Mozart.

Little Sally, resplendent in the blue dress Drewry had made for her, played the part of the model hostess with apparent ease. As instructed by Drewry, she curtsied to the parents of each child, never tugged at her white gloves, and placed her gaily wrapped gifts on the table without appearing too eager to rip them open.

Drewry had to suppress a laugh at the children's earnest good manners, knowing well how impatient they were to get to the fun and games. Even Sam was behaving like a dignified little gentleman.

But learning gentle manners was a requirement for Chase's children, and as their nanny, part of Drewry's job was to see that they received the training that would carry them into adulthood. Now she realized it was also her job to grow into the full maturity of womanhood, herself. Thanks to Matilda, she could now trust God to see her through...once she came clean with Chase.

"There's nothing quite as innocent and full of promise as a little girl's birthday party, is there?"

Chase's deep voice interrupted Drewry's musings. She turned to find herself looking up into his sober gaze. He appeared strained, his chiseled features taut with some unknown burden. Despite the lines of fatigue etched on his face, he was still every bit the consummate master of Magnolia Grange. His flawlessly tailored black jacket hugged broad shoulders that were erect with an air of authority. He was a man accustomed to being in command, she reminded herself, accustomed to respect…not deceit.

I must tell him, Drewry resolved. Remembering Pastor Tillman's sermon and Matilda's wise counsel, she knew it was the right thing, the only thing to do. But she found the prospect of confession frightening. Found his thoroughly masculine presence unnerving as well.

Thinking of his touch the night she so shamelessly thrown herself into his arms, Drewry felt a quickening pulse throbbing in the hollow of her throat. *Whatever possessed you?* she scolded herself. *What must he think of you now?*

She dragged her gaze from his and focused her attention on Sally, playing hostess only a few feet away.

"Is something wrong, Drewry?" he asked kindly. "Is there anything I can do for you?"

Even his voice stirred her senses. "N—no. Well, not exactly. But all the same, I'd like a few moments alone with you, Chase." She forced her voice to remain firm, despite her quivering nerves. Her mind raced. How would she find the words? And how would she handle his obvious disappointment in her? Would he tell her to pack up and leave immediately? If so, where would she go?

"Would the porch be a convenient place?"

"Hmmm?" She started from her reverie. "Oh. Yes. Of course. The porch will be just fine."

Chase lightly held her elbow as he steered her across the room, crowded with children. Even his touch was disturbing. Drewry forced herself to smile and send a reassuring wave to Sally. The child nodded, beaming.

"This party is just what she needed," Drewry said to Chase as they settled onto the same wicker settee where, only an hour or two ago, she'd made her confession to Matilda.

"Yes, our little Sally is becoming quite the poised young lady, thanks to you, I might add." His approving gaze swept her from head to toe. "By the way, Miss Sheffield, did I tell you how lovely you look today? Green becomes you."

The deep timbre of his voice sent a delicious shiver down Drewry's spine. "How thoughtful of you to say so. A woman appreciates a man who notices such things." Again, she couldn't believe she'd been so bold. Whatever was she doing?

Suddenly, their gazes locked. Somewhere nearby, a bird chirped. The scent of roses, mingled with newly mown grass, lay heavy on the humid afternoon air. A feathery wind riffled the leaves on the trees and played in her hair, reminding her of Chase's gentle touch.

Drewry found herself admiring the firm set of his jaw, and longed to reach over and lightly trace the outline of it with her fingertips. She trembled slightly at the memory of how he'd crushed her to his chest, how her hands curled so willingly around those strong shoulders.

But this was no time for idle daydreams. She shook her head to clear it, then returned to the matter at hand. *He deserves to know the truth. I must be honest with him, once and for all. And if I must, why not now?*

Drewry took a deep breath, squared her shoulders, and plunged in. "Chase, there is something I must tell you. A confession, really, and—"

"Papa! Papa!" shouted Sally. Tears streaming down her face, the little girl ran across the terrace toward her father, who leapt to his feet at the first sounds of her distress.

"Sweetheart, what is it?" He dropped onto one knee and gathered her close as the child sobbed convulsively.

"Oh, Papa. They're so mean!"

"Who is mean, sweetheart?"

"Nellie and Cornelia." Sally hiccuped. "They said their daddies call you names. They say you're not a good Virginian. They say you're—you're crazy!"

Chase grinned broadly and whipped out his handkerchief. "Now, now, sweetheart. Don't cry."

"They say you treat the Negroes like reg'lar folks," she said as he dabbed at her tears. "But I don't understand, because *aren't* they reg'lar folks?"

"Yes, Miss Sally Ann Auburn, they most certainly are. And can you tell me why?"

Sally blinked and met his eyes. "'Cause all people are God's children, made in His image. So, we must treat every single person with respect, no matter what color their skin is."

Chase smiled. "That's my girl! You know what's right. Now then, when people think or say cruel things, does that change the truth?"

Sally shook her head. "No, Papa."

Tenderly, Chase pushed an errant curl out of his daughter's eyes. "Then don't ever let anyone make you doubt what's right. What others think doesn't matter; living with integrity is the only way to please the Lord."

"Yes, Papa." Sally looked adoringly at her father, then furrowed her brow in a look of puzzlement. "Papa, what does integrity mean?"

Chase chuckled. "It means honesty, sweetheart. Honesty and purity of heart."

Sally brightened. Stretching on tiptoe to give him a hug, she skipped gaily back to her party.

Chase stood to his full, towering height, putting Drewry in mind of the spruce trees that lined the western edge of the property. "She's growing up far too quickly," he observed.

"Yes." Drewry squirmed uncomfortably in her seat and rose to stand beside him. "Perhaps we should get back to the party."

"Yes. I'm scheduled to referee a croquet game on the lawn once the birthday girl cuts her cake." He turned to leave the terrace, then stopped abruptly. "But wait, didn't you have something important to tell me? A confession, I believe you called it?"

Drewry wondered if he could hear the mad beating of her heart. She clasped her hands together, wishing for a way to forestall the inevitable. But how would she tell him now, especially after the touching scene she just witnessed? "I—I just wanted to tell you...to confess..."

The way he stood there, grinning at her, took Drewry's breath. She began again. "I just wanted to confess how...how very happy I am here, Chase." She swallowed her cowardice like bitter bile. A heavy sense of foreboding fell over her. Integrity in her own life was seriously lacking. How would she ever find the courage to confess that lack to this man who prized the virtue so highly!

Chase hesitated for a moment, as if waiting to hear more.But Drewry kept quiet. Silently, she watched as the sunshine, filtering through a cloud, carving the planes of his face into interesting angles. Her heart sank. How much longer could she go on playing this awful game—with him and with God?

"I'm glad to hear that, Drewry." Gallantly, Chase extended his elbow. "Now, shall we rejoin the party?"

As she tucked her arm into his and walked back into the house, she glanced up at the sky. Somewhere up there, behind that clear blue canvas, the stars twinkled chastely.

She couldn't help wondering, though, how they managed to stay so completely hidden from view.

ELEVEN

*D*ear Miss Drew,

What a wonderful surprise to get another letter from you so soon. Missy and me read it three, four times over.

Things sound mighty exciting down in Richmond, that's for sure. And things here in Freeland is mighty exciting, too. Your uncle and me had us a big clash. He went into town last week, and decide to stop in at the post office to get the mail. He come home from town with the packages and the envelopes, bellowing like a bull. He call me a sneaky snake. Ask me how could I keep your whereabouts a secret, knowing how he be suffering over missing you. Can't tell you where Miss Drew is, I tell him, 'cause I give my word not to. She be scared, I say, that you gonna make her marry old Porter Hopkins.

Mr. James get real quiet. Sit in his big leather chair and start to weep. He say you mean everything to him, since you is practically the only family he got left in all the world. Then he say he gonna quit drinking whiskey. Going to quit gambling, too. I believe it when I see it, I say to myself. Well, it been nearly two *weeks now, and Mr. James ain't touched a drop of whiskey in all this time. Ain't played no cards, neither, far as I can tell.*

Maybe this change be on account of Naomi Joy. Her daddy be the minister over on the Piscataway Reservation. Miss Joy's mama be a Susquehannock Indian, Mr. James tell me. I ain't seen her yet, but your uncle say she more beautiful than a sunrise. He say she have hair the color of the midnight sky and eyes as brown as roasted chestnuts. He say me and Miss Joy has lots in common, since we both half-breeds.

Mr. James, he go to Sunday services and read his Bible every night before bed. Why, he even say a word of thanks before meals, just like we done before the War. Things be about as right as right can get round here, Miss Drew. All this time, I offer up my humble prayers that the Lord would see fit to put the heart and soul back into Mr. James, and though I believed it would happen, I reckoned I'd be long gone before that day come. But praise God, He let me witness the change with my very own eyes!

So don't you worry none about us, Miss Drew. Mr. James say to tell you he loves you, and that he is sorry for all the grief he cause you. He wants to find a way to say so in person, cause he don't want to start his new life with Miss Joy till he sets right all the things he done wrong. I'll wait to hear from you, Miss Drew.

Look like you got lots of hard decisions to make. Telling the whole truth to Mr. Chase and forgiving your uncle ain't gonna be easy. But if the Lord can help your uncle do the right thing, He can sure help you.

Missy and me gonna keep praying for you. And we thank you for your prayers, too. Seems they done a lot of good!

Your friend,
Jeb

Drewry sat, stunned into silence, Jeb's letter in her trembling hands.

So Uncle James wanted reconciliation. Drewry didn't know if she had the strength of character to forgive him. It would be wonderful, she acknowledged, to have him in her life again. Especially if, as Jeb had written, he'd truly given up whiskey and gambling.

She wondered about the woman in Uncle James's life. He'd always been a ladies' man, but not once could she recall a woman who'd inspire a commitment from him. This teacher of the Indians must be special, indeed, if he'd even gone back to church to please her!

"*Mr. James, he say you mean everything to him,*" Drewry read again, "*and he wants to find a way to tell you in person how sorry he be for all the grief he cause you.*"

Drewry's heart beat faster at the thought of Uncle James coming to Richmond. How would she arrange such a meeting? More troubling, how would she explain it to Chase?

Sighing, she carefully tucked Jeb's letter into the wide, curved drawer of her desk. Resting her elbows on its shining surface, Drewry held her head in her hands and closed her eyes. *Why must life be so complicated?*

⌣

The children were asleep in their rooms, taking their afternoon naps, when Drewry, with no duties to perform, wandered down to the kitchen. Maybe she could help Matilda with dinner.

The woman's white teeth gleamed in her broad black face as she handed Drewry a small metal bucket. "Go on down the path yonder," Matilda said, "an' pick me this pail full of blackberries. I'm just about to roll out some dough to make us a pie for dessert."

It would be wonderful to be outdoors—alone—to contemplate the state of her confusing life, Drewry decided. She hitched up the hem of her gray cotton dress and tucked it into the belt at her waist to protect the white lace trim from gathering dust and dirt along the path. And because it was warmer outside than she expected when she put on the high-collared frock, she undid the velvet-covered button at the neckline. Thankfully, she'd wound her hair into a bun and tucked it into a lacy white chignon.

The gentle July breeze cooled her bare neck as she stepped lightly down the beaten path. Jeb's earlier advice—to tell Chase the truth about herself—confirmed Matilda's sentiments before Sally's party about honesty. And Drewry would have confessed, too, if not for Sally's tearful interruption.

Drewry inhaled sharply. *No telling where you'd be right now if you'd gone ahead with it!* Still, it was the right thing to do, and she knew it. *Well, you can tell him later. After he's fully recuperated from the fire....*

The path narrowed as the willowy blackberry branches, bowed under their sweet burden, hung low. For several dozen yards, she plucked the near-black, shining berries and dropped them into the silvery bucket, popping one of the sweet-sour treats into her mouth for every five that hit the bucket's bottom.

She had almost reached the clearing at the far end of the path when she noticed it. Matilda told her that a tiny, rough-hewn chapel sat in the middle of a meadow, but since she'd never traveled this far down the path before, Drewry had never seen it for herself. The peaked roof, shingled with weathered shakes, and the whitewashed half-walls that supported it, glowed warmly in the afternoon sun.

The small building seemed to beckon to her. Leaving the path, she made her way to the door. Inside, where it was cool and shady, two rows of wooden benches lined the earthen floor. Up front, she saw an altar of split rail construction, and high above it, a crude wooden cross, fashioned from sturdy oak branches.

Drewry took a seat on the aisle and tried to picture the chapel the way Matilda described it, decorated with yellow satin bows and bouquets of roses, grown in Chase's hothouse, for the Easter sunrise service. She blinked, and imagined it bedecked with holly and boxwood and crimson poinsettias during the Christmas season.

Near the front of the chapel, running the length of the altar, Drewry noticed the kneeler. She placed her half-filled bucket of berries on the bench and walked purposefully toward it. Then, lifting her skirts, she knelt.

"Take your problems to Jesus, honey lamb," Matilda had said. Folding her hands, Drewry looked up at the cross. "I do not wish to be a deceiver," she prayed earnestly. "Lord, I want nothing more than to confess this horrible sin and beg Chase's forgiveness."

Tears welled up in Drewry's eyes and a sob ached in her throat. *Help me find the strength to do what is right*, she prayed silently. *Give me the wisdom to know when the time is right to tell him the truth.*

In the moments of silence that followed, Drewry experienced a calming of her spirit such as she'd never known. She felt certain that this peace was the Lord's way of telling her that He would show her when and where to make her full confession.

Pleased with her decision to follow God's leading, she stood, grabbed her berry bucket, and headed for the path that led back to the manor house. Halfway there, as she picked more berries, Drewry thought she heard a masculine sound, as if someone were clearing his throat, somewhere to the north of the path.

She parted the low-growing foliage to peer into the field beyond, and saw Chase standing alone in the middle of the flower-filled meadow. Because he seemed so deep in thought, Drewry was concerned that her sudden appearance might startle him. Besides, he looked so forlorn that he was sure to be embarrassed if she joined him without warning.

Quietly, Drewry backed up a few steps, then made her way forward again, making as much noise as possible.

"Who's there?" he called.

"It's Drewry." Only then did she allow him to see her peeking through the bushes. "Chase, what are you doing way out here?"

In a few long strides, he was beside her on the path, beneath a canopy of pine, maple, and birch branches. "I was asking the Lord's guidance in finding a new field to test my plants," he said, smiling. "And what brings *you* all this way from the house?"

"The children are napping, so I'm helping Matilda." Drewry held her bucket out for him to see. "As Sam might say, I'm on a berry important mission—dessert!"

Chase threw back his head and laughed heartily. "Well, I'm 'berry' impressed."

The music of his laughter echoed through the meadow.

Drewry feigned hurt feelings. "You find me amusing, Mr. Auburn?"

He met her gaze, his smile fading as he stepped closer. "I find you...irresistible." With no warning whatsoever, he pulled her close. "You smell like lilacs," he sighed into her ear.

Strong hands smoothed her hair. Then, gently, trembling fingertips caressed her cheeks. Drewry had never seen a look more loving and tender than the one emanating from his dark eyes.

With one forefinger, he tilted her head, then bent to touch her lips with his...feather-light at first, then longer and stronger until their breath mingled and it seemed there was no air anywhere in the universe but the air they shared. This was nothing like the kiss she'd given him on the night of the fire. It seemed to surge upward from the very depths of his soul, as if something long-buried in his heart was straining to break free.

She responded with her own soft sighs. "Chase," she murmured against his lips. "Oh, Chase..."

And then, just as easily, it seemed, as he captured her in the powerful circle of his embrace, Chase held her at arm's length and groaned. The mournful sound of it shattered the beautiful, magical moment. Pain glittered icily where warmth had glowed in his eyes. Without another word, he turned away, then stomped down the path.

For a moment only, she allowed herself to believe that he might really care for her. *Silly girl*, she reminded herself, *unrequited love is as much as you can hope for with a man like Chase Auburn.* At least she'd have that moment—the sweet sensation of his lips against hers and the sound of his soft endearments in her ear—to remember for the rest of her days.

She stood alone on the path for a long time, unable to explain Chase's sudden departure. A squirrel, scampering in the branches overhead, roused her from her reverie. But even its comical antics and the shower of wild nuts it rained down upon her failed to produce a smile.

Woodenly, Drewry headed for the house, too stunned even to weep.

TWELVE

She hadn't slept a wink. The clock on her mantel told her it was nearly two in the morning.

Drewry paced her room, palms cupping elbows as she gnawed at her lower lip. No matter how many times she replayed the tender scene in the woods, she couldn't understand why Chase had left her standing there alone.

She went over every moment of their interlude time and again, asking herself if perhaps she'd offended him in some way. But no, each time the lovely picture presented itself, Drewry was forced to admit that nothing unpleasant had occurred. Chase had taken her in his arms as easily as he took breath, his gentle voice caressing her ears with words of endearment. And his lips, surrounded by the thick handlebar mustache, had sought hers so sweetly.

She hadn't stiffened, nor had she behaved wantonly. Rather, she'd praised God for blessing her with proof that Chase felt about her as she did about him. The prayer had been short, however, for even before Drewry concluded, Chase cut the kiss short.

He'd seemed angry, no, *furious* more accurately described his mood when he made his abrupt departure. One moment, she was surrounded by two strong, loving arms; the next, she was standing alone and bewildered on the path.

Drewry stopped her pacing and took a deep breath. When it failed to cleanse her mind and soul of the deep ache inside, she stepped out onto the balcony. There, in the muggy night air, she stared into the inky sky. The stars glittered from their velvety background. Drewry picked out the Big Dipper and Orion. Sea captains set the course of their ships by looking into this same sky, Drewry knew. But what made them trust that those far-off sparkling diamonds would lead them safely from port to port, and home again? What did they see up there in the heavens that she didn't?

Suddenly, though she was surrounded by the vast sky above Magnolia Grange, Drewry felt closed in. Suffocated. Smothered.

Hurrying inside, she wrapped a plain black skirt around her white nightdress, then draped a fringed scarf around her shoulders. Her unbound hair flowed down her back like a nutmeg mane as she ran silently through the hall, down the grand staircase, across the foyer.

The moment her feet made contact with the rough, cool bricks of the front porch, she smiled, glad she hadn't bothered with boots. The soft coolness of the freshly cut lawn felt comforting against her bare feet. She took her time getting from the front to the side yard, stopping now and then to wiggle her toes in the grass. The delicate scent of roses grew stronger as she neared the terrace.

Never in her months at Magnolia Grange had she been so bold as to pluck one, unless instructed to do so by Matilda. But the petals, glowing like white velvet in the moonlight, invited her to cherish their beauty, and Drewry gave in to the temptation. The blossom broke off more easily than she anticipated, and surprisingly, the thorns did her no harm.

She sat on the iron bench that wrapped around the maple nearest the terrace. Stroking the flower against her cheek, Drewry closed her eyes. Its silken petals reminded her of Chase's tender caress just before he lowered his head to hers that very afternoon. Her newly kissed lips now nuzzled the satiny bloom. *Why did you leave me that way, Chase?*

Drewry opened her eyes, surprised at the tears that blurred her vision. Surely there were no more tears left....

Then something near the barn caught her attention—something that glowed round and red, like the tip of a hot poker. She blinked, and it was gone. Drewry continued to stare at the spot for a moment longer, certain that all her exhaustive crying caused a temporary lack of sanity.

But no...there it was again. And much closer this time.

She could smell it now, too. It was a cigar, like those that had clouded the air in Joshua Taylor's office, and the ones that fogged the dining room whenever Uncle James brought his gambling cronies home to play poker.

"You look mighty pretty sitting there in the moonlight," said a deep, rasping voice.

Drewry jumped to her feet and stifling a scream, cowered near the trunk of the tree.

"Take care with that rose now," he cautioned. "Pretty as they are, those thorns can leave a nasty scratch."

Finally, she found her voice. "Come out of the shadows and show yourself."

"Happy to oblige, pretty lady." The rotund figure of Sheriff Alden Kelly stepped into view.

Drewry wished now that she *had* screamed—screamed for all she was worth. "What are you doing here at this hour?" she demanded, hoping he wouldn't hear the fear trembling in her voice.

His grating laughter struck a deeper terror. "Why don't you tell me why you think I'm here." He took several steps nearer, so near she could see her tiny reflection in the black pinpoints of his pupils.

Though Drewry stood tall, the top of her head barely reached his shoulder. "You've no business here," she said firmly. "And if you don't leave at once, I'll call Mister Au—"

In seconds, Kelly was all around her, it seemed, as one hand snaked out and grabbed her wrist and the other clamped over her mouth. "You won't be callin' anybody, Miss High and Mighty." The sheriff started dragging her in the direction of the barn, scraping her bare feet and gashing her ankles on the flagstone path.

Drewry kicked, pulled at his forearms, pitched her body to and fro, and screamed against his sweaty, cigar-stinking palm.

"Now that's what I like," he said, chuckling under his breath. "A scrappy young thing that'll make it worth fightin' for."

A paralyzing fear nearly choked off her breath. Surely he didn't mean to…

When Kelly shoved her into the dark, hay-strewn barn, Drewry took a deep breath and opened her mouth to scream. "I wouldn't do that if I were you," he warned, his voice flowing sweet and slow as maple syrup in February.

She heard the unmistakable click of a pistol hammer locking into position, and pressed her trembling lips together.

"So she's smart as well as strong," Kelly said, nodding approvingly. "Good. Don't believe I've ever had me a smart woman before."

"You won't get away with this," she said, backing away. "Someone will see or hear…"

Now she was against the wall of the barn. There was nowhere else to go.

"I've been here often enough to know this place almost as well as I know my own. Nobody stirs 'round here at night. 'Specially after midnight." The man's evil snicker hung heavy on the humid air. "Guess you rich folks need all the beauty sleep you can get, eh?"

Drewry decided that no matter what happened, Sheriff Alden Kelly would know he'd been in a fight! She leaned against the rough wooden wall, watching...waiting...

Here now! What was that pressing into her spine?

Slipping her hand slowly behind her back, Drewry wrapped it around the handle of the pitchfork that hung on a peg just inside the door. If she were careful, very careful...

Kelly moved to the right. He hadn't lied. Obviously, he had been here often. How else would he have known precisely where the lantern hung? "Just a tad of light," he whispered, "for atmosphere."

She waited until he lifted the globe and struck the match before turning to seize her weapon. The leather strap by which it hung held it higher on the wall than she thought. Drewry tugged, lifted, tugged again, and still she wasn't able to get it down in one, fluid movement.

"Yes, indeedy," Kelly said, unhitching the pitchfork for her. "I do like 'em scrappy." He tossed the tool aside, and it landed with a quiet thump on the floor of an empty stall.

Before she knew what was happening, Drewry was flat on her back on a bed of straw, looking up helplessly into the fat, leering face of Alden Kelly. The lantern cast a dim, eerie glow around the barn's interior, reminding Drewry of the haunted house the youth in her community created one Halloween.

Again Kelly clamped a greasy palm over her mouth. Using one knee to pin her right arm to the floor, the other kept her left arm in place. "Yes, indeedy," he said again, showing her his gap-toothed grin, "I do like 'em scrappy." Then, with his free hand, he grabbed the collar of her nightdress.

Chase! she screamed silently. *Chase, where are you?*

❧

He'd been back and forth across the floor dozens of times, and considered it a minor miracle that his pacing hadn't worn a path in the rug. Chase stepped out onto his balcony and leaned his palms against the picket rail. *You've lost your mind, man,* he said to himself. *Whatever possessed you to kiss her that way?*

But he knew the answer to that question.

Drewry inspired the kiss. And she'd done it simply by being herself. How wonderful she had felt in his arms. How sweetly she melted against him, yielding to his tender kiss. He'd thoroughly enjoyed the embrace, the soft whispering sounds of her sighs. But the image of Theresa suddenly entered his head, blotting out all rational thought. It didn't matter that his wife had told him in plain language that she wanted him to find another wife. It didn't matter that Claib and Matilda and Pastor Tillman had explained, time and again, that not even God expected him to remain alone once Theresa was gone.

But it was something Pastor Tillman said at the cemetery that echoed round and round in his head: "You'll be reunited with her in paradise…." How could Chase rejoin Theresa in heaven after he'd been with another woman on earth?

Yes, he'd read it in the Bible for himself: heaven was completely unlike earth. There would be no marriages there. Mark 12:25 explained it perfectly: *"For when they shall rise from the dead, they neither marry, nor are given in marriage; but are as the angels which are in heaven."* Still, Chase could not bring himself to begin a new romance. Not even with a woman as wonderful as Drewry Sheffield.

Matilda knew her charge well, and had placed an iron lawn chair on his balcony. Chase sat and propped his feet on the table beside it, and, leaning back, closed his eyes. A sense of unease, like none he ever felt before, settled over him. He opened his eyes and stared into the starry sky.

He could have sworn he heard Drewry's voice.

Yes…there it was again. And she was calling his name.

Chase sat up, straining to hear. A second passed, then two. Though he heard nothing, the sense that she needed him wrapped around his chest like an iron band, tightening as the seconds continued to tick silently by.

Standing, Chase peered across the dew-dampened yard. He continued to glance to and fro, until his gaze rested upon the barn, some hundred yards in the distance. *Is that a light in the window?* he wondered, squinting. *Some fool has left a lantern burning!*

The very idea alarmed Chase. After witnessing firsthand the quick destructiveness of fire, he had no desire to see the scene repeated. He dashed down the stairs, not even bothering to close the front door behind him, and ran toward the dim glow.

He had but a dozen yards to go when he heard scuffling sounds. Claib had moved the horses to an outbuilding near the servants' cottages, so that he could repair the roof, damaged in the last thunderstorm. Since no animals boarded there, the noises confused Chase. Perhaps a cat or a family of field mice….

Chase stopped dead in his tracks and keened his ear toward the barn doors. *That's a man's voice!* Though Chase couldn't make out what the fellow was saying, the throaty, guttural laughter made it patently clear that he was up to no good.

That's when he heard for the first time the soft, muffled cries of a woman. *Drewry!*

Everything in him told him to barge in and lift the man by his hair, then beat the living daylights out of him. If she was harmed in any way…

But Chase knew better than to rush in without a plan. Whoever held her there against her will would no doubt react in violence if he felt threatened.

Chase must plan his strategy well. But he had to work quickly.

Sneaking around to the back side of the barn, he peered through the filmy window. There, on his hands and knees, was

Alden Kelly. And beneath him, Drewry cried and thrashed about for dear life.

Chase would go in through the side door. Claib had constructed a wooden hallway of sorts just inside, to keep the cows immobile during branding. An assortment of iron tools would be within easy reach. Chase stepped softly to avoid making a sound that might warn Kelly of his approach.

Slowly, he slipped in through the narrow opening. Just as he expected, iron bars and rods hung by leather thongs on the barn wall. Chase eased one from its wooden peg and bit his lip, as if doing so would assure his silence.

Then he made his move.

"Turn her loose, Kelly!"

The sheriff, red-faced and sweating, turned toward the sound of Chase's voice. "Well," he said to Drewry, "what have we here? Your boss man has warm feelings for you, does he?"

"He's got a gun, Chase!" she warned, her words muffled by the pressure of Kelly's palm. "Go away. Please! Run!" Her wild gaze implored Chase to leave the barn. "Go!" she muttered. "Think of the children, Chase!"

Chase lunged forward. Somehow, miraculously, he stood behind Kelly, gripping the branding iron with both hands... against the lout's throat.

Kelly sputtered and choked, but refused to let go of Drewry. Grabbing a handful of her hair, he pulled her with him as Chase lifted him off his feet. "Turn me loose or I'll shoot her right before your very eyes!"

Chase's gaze sought Drewry's. *I'll do whatever he asks to save you*, he seemed to be saying as he dropped the tool.

In that instant, Kelly managed to wriggle free of Chase's hold, dropping his pistol in the process. But he still had Drewry—his ticket to freedom. Kelly lifted the lighted lantern high in his free hand. "I'll make ya a deal, Auburn."

Chase stood, fists doubled at his sides, glaring at him.

"Let me leave here with the girl, and I won't make an orphan of your young'uns."

Chase pictured Sam and Sally, innocent and vulnerable. They'd only be more so if anything happened to him. But if he didn't take a firm stand, here and how, it was only a matter of time before Kelly and his kind made orphans of them, anyway.

"Your stubbornness will be the end of you yet, Auburn." Kelly removed a stick of dynamite from the back pocket of his trousers as Drewry tried to hold the bodice of her torn gown closed with the other.

"Gotta have somethin'exciting to tell the boys about my visit here tonight," he said with a wink. "You have 'til the count of ten to back off, *way* off, 'cause I aim to blow this fancy barn of yours to smithereens."

Chase glanced at the pistol, lying on the floor near Kelly's feet. "Don't even think about it, Auburn," Kelly said, stooping to retrieve it.

"You'll never get away with this, Kelly."

"Yes, I will," he said, tucking the revolver into his belt, "and we both know it. Now get on outta here unless you want to go sky high right along with your barn." He withdrew a kitchen match from his shirt pocket. Holding Drewry as a shield, he walked backward, waving the dynamite and the match in his free hand.

Halfway from the stall to the door, he tripped over the branding iron Chase had dropped. When he landed spread eagle on the hay-strewn floor, he ignited the match with his thumbnail.

"Run, Drewry, run!" Chase hollered as Kelly began the countdown.

As she scrambled toward the door, Chase noticed her bloodied, bruised feet. He didn't waste a moment, but scooped her up in his arms and ran with her toward the house.

Kelly was on his knees by the time he yelled, "Seven, eight, nine!"

Something must have gone terribly wrong, Chase knew. That fuse had been no less than two feet long, yet suddenly, Kelly's grating laughter was drowned out by the dynamite's detonation. Boards and nails flew in all directions. Chase, fearing a shard might gore Drewry, pushed her to the ground and threw himself on top of her.

A bloodcurdling bellow punctuated the blast. Chase lifted his head in time to see Sheriff Alden Kelly, staggering wide-eyed around the barnyard, clutching his barrel chest: The force of the blast had driven a large sword-shaped splinter of wood directly through his heart.

He was dead before he hit the ground.

❧

Drewry held the mug in both trembling hands as she Matilda draped a quilt around her shoulders. "I'm fine," she insisted around swollen lips. "Really. All this fuss and bother is unnecessary."

"Nonsense, girl," the big woman said. "You is gonna drink that milk, then you is gonna climb into bed and get some shut-eye."

She hadn't been able to argue when Matilda insisted on drawing her a hot bath, half an hour ago, and Drewry didn't imagine she'd be able to argue this point, either. She smiled feebly. "Thank you. Thank you all."

"No thanks necessary," Claib said. "You is family, Miss Drew, an' we take good care of our own."

Chase hadn't said much since she'd hobbled into the kitchen. It had been a stupid, foolish thing to go outside alone in the dark. She knew that now. "But goin' outdoors with no shoes on," Matilda scolded, hands propped on her beefy hips, "in the dead o' night when you can't see where you is goin'?" The woman could only shake her head. "What was you thinkin', Miss Drewry?"

Drewry stared at her reflection on the surface of the milk. "I don't know," she fibbed.

She knew exactly what she'd been thinking: Why had Chase so callously left her there on the path after their passionate embrace?

In the tub earlier, memory of the kiss paled by comparison to the fact that he'd put his life on the line for her! Sacrificed his barn—and all the tools in it—*for her!*

The image of Alden Kelly, gripping the bloody stake that ended his life, made her shudder.

Chase was beside her in an instant. Gently, he used a dampened towel to dab at the cuts on her face. Holding her gaze, he said "Did he...did he hurt you?"

She knew what he was *really* asking. "No," she said. *But he would have, if you hadn't shown up when you did.* "He did me no lasting harm, thanks to you."

"Thank God," he said, pressing the cloth to her forehead.

"I'm fine. Really," she insisted, waving him away.

But he refused to obey. "We almost lost you tonight, Drewry. I'm so very grateful the good Lord heard my prayers."

She looked at him then—at the soulful brown eyes and the worried brow. At the tense set of his powerful jaw. "You...you *prayed* for me?"

Chase snorted. "Well of course I did! You mean so very much to—to all of us here at Magnolia Grange."

Had he hesitated because he couldn't admit that she meant something to him? Her heart soared at the mere possibility.

"It's time you get on up to bed, Miss Drew," Matilda ordered. "Mr. Chase, you want Claib an' Simon to carry her, so's she don't have to walk on them poor feet?"

Chase stood and dropped the bloodied towel into the dry sink. "No. I'll take her up."

Matilda didn't seem at all surprised by his answer. With a huff and a puff, she relieved Drewry of her mug. "Y'all get on outta here now," she said to Claib and Simon. "The rooster be crowin' mighty early in the mornin', an' I ain't gonna ring the breakfast bell more'n once!"

Ignoring Matilda's flapdoodle, Chase gently slipped one arm behind Drewry's knees, the other behind her back, and lifted her from the chair. "You'll tell me if I hurt you…"

She wrapped her arms around his neck. "You wouldn't hurt me, Chase Auburn," she said, not with an air of arrogance, but with an inner certainty. "You couldn't hurt anyone."

"Oh now? I would have killed Kelly tonight," he said, climbing the stairs as he cradled her in his arms like a rare treasure.

Drewry shook her head. "You'd have hurt him, maybe. But you'd never have killed him. At least, not on purpose."

Chase smiled. "And how is it you think you know me so well?"

Their lips were mere inches apart. If she leaned forward just a bit, she could close that gap and kiss him. But she didn't dare. Not after the way he'd behaved that afternoon. *Oh, but I don't know you*, she thought, swallowing a sob. *And I doubt I ever shall.*

～

Long after he gently closed her bedchamber door, Drewry laid awake, her mind whirling. She was sure Chase didn't love her… at least, not the way a man loves a woman; Matilda and Claib had been dead wrong about that! But he did care about her. That much was evident in the cautious way he'd tended her injuries, in the gentle way he'd carried her upstairs, in the sweetness of his smile as he blew out the light.

She took a deep breath and stretched out under the covers. *Some folks live a lifetime without experiencing one true-blue friendship,* she told herself as she closed her eyes. *If nothing else, Chase is your friend. Be thankful for that much.*

It wouldn't keep her from wishing their relationship could be more. She'd promised Matilda that she would behave like a grown-up. And she would begin tomorrow. No more hangdog expressions. No more solitary pouting sessions. No more wishing upon the stars for what could never be.

Drewry wasn't happy about the fact that Chase would never be more than a good and loving friend, but surprisingly, the fact didn't distress her, either. He'd saved her virtue *and* her life tonight!

Thank You, God, she prayed, *for sending Chase to the barn to save me from that awful man. And be merciful to Alden Kelly....*

Yes, Chase's behavior was proof that he was—and always would be—a trusted friend. He deserved to hear the truth, and tomorrow, he *would*.

The decision lulled her, and for the first time in days, Drewry slept—the deep, contented slumber of a child.

THIRTEEN

Chase paced back and forth, his booted footsteps echoing on the hardwood floor. At this late hour, his library provided welcome solitude. The only light came from the moon, burnishing the room with ethereal whiteness. He needed privacy to mull over the night's strange events and to seek divine guidance for his confused feelings.

Memories lingered to haunt him; the hurt that ripped across Drewry's countenance when he pushed her away this afternoon; her anguish and terror when he burst into the barn and interrupted Alden Kelly's shameful business. Drewry's pleading cries that, even now, tore at his heart...the stench of dynamite, the heat of the blazing barn....

A barn could be replaced. Drewry's honor could not, and he thanked God that he'd arrived in time to spare her....

Chase stopped pacing and ran his hand through his thick, dark hair, his thoughts churning. He took a deep breath and looked out the window, toward the shadow of the trees, where Kelly had met his end. For a man who usually knew his own feelings as well as he knew his name, Chase had to admit he was stumped. He hadn't planned on kissing Drewry earlier in the day, but at the time, the action seemed so right. So natural. If he hadn't thought of Theresa....

But it was the violence of his emotions in the barn that shook him to the core.

The great wellspring of fury he'd felt for Drewry's assailant, the urge to protect her—an urge which would have driven him to throw himself into Kelly's line of fire if necessary—went far beyond the duty of employer to employee. This much he knew.

Emotions of such magnitude rightly belonged to a husband, whose holy vow it was to protect and honor his beloved wife, even at the cost of his own life. But the instant he realized the danger Drewry was in, white-hot rage rose involuntarily from the depths of his being. Nobody would hurt her, not while there was breath in his body!

Chase sank into the big brown chair beside the fireplace and buried his face in his hands. He was not Drewry's husband. He was *Theresa's* husband.

Painfully, he lifted his head and forced himself to focus on the empty chair opposite his. Theresa's chair. Since her arrival at Magnolia Grange, however, it was Drewry's choice of seating. Now, it was rightfully hers. She earned that place. Night after night, she'd sat there, keeping him company, sharing the rearing of his children, listening as he shared the most private thoughts of his mind, and sometimes, the secrets of his heart.

Ah, yes. *Secrets.*

Miss Drewry Sheffield was definitely guarding some secret. Chase knew it. He could feel it, deep in his bones. She either wouldn't, or couldn't, share the whole truth about herself and her past with him. That hurt him so deeply that it surprised him. Slowly, it dawned on him that his pain at her lack of trust came only because he wanted so badly to share her life—the good and the bad—as completely as only a husband could.

Chase sprang to his feet, strode over to the hearth, and leaned wearily against the massive, carved mantelpiece. Retrieving Theresa's picture from his pocket, he studied it. How could he be a husband to Drewry while in his mind, he was still married to Theresa? He turned the ferrotype over and read the message Theresa inscribed there: "Until death do us part."

Strange that he hadn't thought of that particular part of his marriage vows since the moment he spoke them. Death had seemed so remote and impossible on their wedding day, a day filled with the promise of life. Now he wondered why Theresa had chose that phrase above all the others to write on this picture. Suddenly, he had the sensation that she was reaching back to him, gently untying the knot that bound him to her.

Until death do us part. Tears filled his eyes, and he stared at the words until they blurred. Death had parted them, but Chase had refused to let go.

He closed his eyes and pressed the picture against his chest. "Thank you, Theresa, for the love we shared and for the beautiful children you gave me," he said softly. "You have preceded me to the next life, my darling. If Drewry will have me, I will cherish you no less."

Chase sighed heavily, feeling a weight lift from his heart. He remembered Theresa's last wifely admonition—to find a new love—and he smiled. How well she had known him. How well she loved him!

Reverently, he kissed her likeness and set the picture on the mantelpiece, propped against a vase of marigolds and irises that Sally had arranged for him that morning. He admired the smiling face and felt that Theresa was bestowing her blessing.

He threw himself into his chair and for a long time, gazed at the cold gray ashes in the grate. It warmed his heart to know that

Drewry was safely asleep, upstairs in her bed, drugged slightly by one of Matilda's herbal teas. Soon, he would reveal the depth of his feelings for her. But first, she must trust him enough to share her secret.

Yes, he'd wait, as patiently and expectantly as he waited for the seedlings to break through the fertile soil into the sunlight, because love needed to be grounded in trust.

Besides—and he chuckled softly in anticipation—how bad could his Lady Nanny's secret be?

Freeland, Maryland
August 16, 1868

Dear Miss Drewry,
May the Lord be praised!
Ain't nothing too hard for our God to accomplish. His deeds are truly wondrous to behold. I'm talking about your uncle. Just like the Prodigal Son, he done come back to the Lord.

It has lots to do with Miss Joy and her preacher daddy, but Mister James ain't coming back just to please his lady friend. No siree. He come back to the Lord in his heart. He be a changed man, Miss Drew, a new creature in Christ.

Yesterday, he tell me the truth about who I am. I always suspected, but I never knowed for sure. Me and Mister James, we have the same daddy, Abraham Sheffield! Mister James showed me proof—papers that ole Abe left behind. It explains why you say so many times that I look like Abe when I smile. Me and Mister James is half brothers! He say he ain't ashamed to be related to a black. He say we is all God's children. Well, if me and Mister James is kin, you and me is kin, too! I couldn't love you more, kin or no kin. But I think you already knowed that.

Truth is a powerful healing thing. It sets the soul free. Give your Mr. Chase a chance to prove that he is a good Christian. Tell him the truth, and set yourself free.

Forgive this ole man for rambling and preaching so, but you is my niece, girl, and I only want what is best for you.

Your affectionate uncle,

Jeb Sheffield

P.S. Mister James be planning to travel to Richmond to meet you and patch things up. I know he cause you a passel of grief, but remember, we is to forgive others as we has been forgiven.

⟿

Drewry reread Jeb's letter four times during the carriage ride into Richmond. Things had been happening so quickly, her mind was a blur. The letter arrived only hours before James's telegraph, inviting her to afternoon tea at the Chesterfield Hill Hotel.

Her grip on the letter tightened. Tears welled in her eyes. She'd gained two uncles, all in one day! Dear Jeb! Why, she'd loved him like an uncle, even before the proof was uncovered. And James...*changed?* Could she dare believe that God had given him back to her...the Uncle James, upon whom she could always rely?

She tucked the letter into her purse and withdrew her shopping list. Not wanting to tell Chase that she was meeting Uncle James, she'd written it as an excuse to go into town. Not that Chase would mind her meeting her uncle—of that she had no doubt—but she wasn't yet ready to tell him about her past.

As she swept into the grand lobby of the Chesterfield, with its imposing marble staircase, thick red carpets, enormous chandeliers and stately, high ceilings, Drewry absorbed the elegance that seemed to permeate every inch of the hotel. The manager ushered her into the private parlor where, he informed her, Mr. James Sheffield awaited her.

Leaning on his cane, James stood the moment she appeared in the doorway. Drewry gasped and blinked back the tears that suddenly flooded her eyes. A clean, handsome, sober man with a neatly trimmed black beard stood before her. A man whose clear blue eyes twinkled with the warmth and good humor she remembered so well from childhood. A man who respectfully waited for her gesture of greeting...and forgiveness.

"Uncle James!" Ignoring all ladylike reserve, she threw down her purse and flew to him.

"Ah, my precious Drew-girl," he said, opening his arms as she flung herself against him. "Thank the Lord! I was afraid you wouldn't show up. I certainly don't deserve it after the way I treated you."

Drewry pulled back, just a little, to look up into his eyes and to touch his soft, dark beard. "Oh, Uncle," she sighed. "How could I not forgive you? I *love* you!"

Tears shimmered in his sky-blue eyes. "Thank you," he said softly, shaking his head. "God knows I don't deserve it, but by His grace, I'll never do you wrong again. And that's a promise."

Drewry gazed helplessly at him, dazed by happiness, until they were interrupted by an elderly waiter in a long black morning coat. "Tea is served," he announced stiffly.

Offering his arm to Drewry, James gave a little nod. "Shall we? A toast to forgiveness—with nothing stronger than tea and cream, of course."

He led her to the small, round table in front of the window of their private room. The delicacy of the lace tablecloth, the gleam of the silver, the white translucence of the china—none of this beauty could add one whit to the joy in Drewry's heart. Her cup was overflowing already!

"I have so much to explain," James said as he passed her the silver tray, lined with cucumber sandwiches.

"You needn't explain," she began.

James held up a hand to silence her. "Yes, I must, Drew-girl. As part of my new life in Christ, I want to make things right with you—to confess my...deception."

Her eyes grew round. "Deception?"

James steepled his hands, took a deep breath, and focused on Drewry's face. "This is not an easy thing to admit, but I'm not the war hero everyone thinks I am."

Drewry found herself fiddling nervously with the embroidered trim along the edge of her napkin. "Oh?"

"I deserve a medal alright—for ingenuity in cowardice." He took a deep, shuddering breath. "My last battle, all my men were dying around me. After the shot to my head, I fell, and, like the coward I was, I stayed down and played dead."

Drewry studied her uncle's face. She saw pain there, but not the kind of crazed pain she'd witnessed during his drunken ramblings. This pain was different—serene, hopeful—because it knew forgiveness.

James cleared his throat and continued. "I was wounded, as you know." Unconsciously, his hand strayed to the jagged scar on his face. "But this foot wound...well, that wasn't the result of a Yankee bullet."

Drewry blinked. "It wasn't?"

"No." He dropped his gaze, unable to meet her eyes. "I'm afraid I'll have to take credit for that one. I took out my pistol and shot myself, so there'd be no questions asked."

Without a moment's hesitation, Drewry reached across the table and placed her hand on his. "Oh, Uncle James...." Her heart went out to him. How he must have suffered all these years.

"That's not the worst of it," he admitted sadly. "After I did it, one of my men, dying beside me, struggled to turn his head toward me. He managed to choke out only three words...no more. But those three words have echoed in my mind all these years—haunting, accusing..."

Drewry nodded encouragingly, still clinging to his hand. "What did he say?"

"It's not what he said, but what he asked me...." James's voice trailed off, and he took a deep breath before continuing his painful story. "His last words were, 'How could you?'"

Suddenly, James looked older than his years.

"So maybe you can see now why I tried to escape into the bottle. I'm not excusing my behavior, mind you, but it's important that you understand *why* I did the things I did. I couldn't live with my conscience. Couldn't live with the lie."

It was Drewry's turn to drop her head as Uncle James talked on, venting his years of guilt and frustration.

Drewry's eyes sparkled with unshed tears. She understood so much now...about her uncle...about herself. But "Uncle James...," was all she could manage to say.

"God is merciful," he said, brightening a bit. "He sent a messenger of mercy in the form of Joy, my beautiful Indian princess. She brought me the love and forgiveness of God." James smiled, his eyes filling with light. "But that's another story. Today, I only wanted to tell you the ugly truth about myself and beg your forgiveness. Will you, Drew-girl? Can you ever forgive me?"

She swallowed hard. The nibbles she'd taken of her cucumber sandwich felt like rocks in her throat. "I'm so sorry for the pain you've lived with. Of course, I forgive you, Uncle." She smiled a watery smile. "And I'm happy that you told me the truth. That took great courage..." *More courage than I have*, Drewry admitted to herself.

James squeezed her hand gratefully. "Believe me, Drew-girl, waiting to see how you'd take the news was far more painful than telling it. My worst fear was that I'd lost my little niece forever, especially after that Porter Hopkins stunt." He looked away, shaking his head sadly. "I still can't believe I could have done such a vile and despicable thing."

"Neither can I."

At that, he glanced up. "It was a shameful thing to do…to take a beautiful, intelligent girl like you and…" He broke off with a sigh. "Well, you deserve the best man God ever created, not some oaf like Hopkins." James chuckled in spite of himself. "You should have seen him when I told him you'd run off. His face turned as red as a pot of stewed beet roots. I thought he'd die of a stroke right there and then!"

Drewry grinned. "I wish I could have been around to see that!" After a short pause, she added, "It all seems so silly now." Then she asked the question she'd been wondering since receiving his invitation. "However did you get back the deed to Plumtree Orchards?"

"Old Jeb to the rescue, of course. He called the minister, who called the judge, and we worked things out. "I was out of my mind back then! What can I do to make it up to you?"

She shook her head. "Having you back in my life—the way you were before—is an answer to prayer."

James winked. "I promise never to gamble you away again. But I'll gladly give you away…to the bridegroom of your choice! Now, what's this I hear about a handsome employer?"

Drewry shifted nervously on the tufted, velvet-cushioned chair. "He's handsome, all right. Brave enough to stand up to a gang of Klansmen, yet gentle enough to be a loving father." She averted her gaze, and focused on the candelabra on the fireplace mantel across the room. "But I don't know that he cares for me… romantically, that is."

"Drew-girl, any man who'd pass you up has got to be as crazy as I was on the night I gambled you away."

Drewry met his loving gaze and smiled sadly. "Tell me about Jeb," she said, trying to steer the conversation away from Chase and his obvious lack of interest in her. "How did he react when he discovered that Grandfather was his daddy?"

"His feet haven't touched the ground since I told him we're half brothers," James said, smiling.

"You knew all this time, and didn't tell him?"

His face flushed dark red beneath the black beard. "Yes, though I'm ashamed to admit it."

"But, Uncle, you always told me the truth when I was a child. Don't you remember when Muffin died? You were the only one who was honest with me. And what about when Mama and Papa were killed? Only you would tell me what really happened."

"Yes, yes, I remember," he said hastily. "But you see, Drewry, I told you the truth, because it was an easy truth. It's easy to explain to a little girl that her puppy died. But it's harder to come clean about family secrets and personal inadequacy. Jeb, for one, my assigning officer, for another...." He cleared his throat. "I should have told Jeb the truth about his parentage, should have admitted to my assigning officer that I didn't have the experience to lead men in battle. But, in both cases, my pride stood in the way. I'm afraid I went for cheap honesty, instead."

"Cheap honesty?" Drewry echoed in surprise.

"Honesty that didn't cost me much." James cracked a grin that reached all the way to his clear blue eyes. "Yeah, cheap honesty can make a fellow feel downright self-righteous. Hardly the kind of honesty Christ was talking about."

Cheap honesty. The concept stirred something deep within Drewry. It was easy to be honest with Sally and Sam. They were children, after all, and gave their trust so freely. But to be honest with Chase when she could risk losing him—losing almost everything and everyone she had come to love—well, *that* was honesty of a more expensive variety, to be sure.

"Uncle James," she began, leaning forward earnestly, "I'd like to ask your advice about a situation I find myself in—a situation where cheap honesty just isn't good enough..."

FOURTEEN

Autumn came early to Richmond that year, bringing with it chilly evenings and brisk mornings. Drewry was forced to begin giving Sally and Sam their lessons inside, much to their dismay.

On one particularly cool October afternoon, however, Drewry suggested they take their "classroom" outside once again, where they could pick up leaf samples from those that blanketed the lawn. There, sitting on a thick patchwork quilt Drewry spread on the ground, they discussed plant structure and construction. She taught the children that pigments, developing in the cells of the leaves, and decomposition of chlorophyll, caused the red and yellow and orange colors, and that every leaf leaves a scar when it falls from the tree.

Sally was amazed by the phenomenon. "But, Drewry," she said, looking up at the still-leafy branches overhead, "there are millions and millions of leaves on those trees!"

Drewry nodded her agreement.

"Oh!" the child exclaimed. "The poor trees! That means they'll have millions and millions of scars!"

Sam seemed disturbed by the information and reminded Drewry how he fell out of his red wagon the week before, scraping both knees on the flagstone walk that bordered the house. "Doo-ree," he said, placing his tiny hand in hers, "when the leafs fall off, does it hurt the trees?"

Drewry smiled and gently stroked his cheek. "No, not a bit."

Tentatively, he touched each brown scab. "I started to peel one," he began, wincing at the memory, "but it hurted. Matilda said if I tooked it off, it would leave a scar." He stood up again. "If it hurted me to get a scar, why wouldn't it hurt the trees?"

"Because, dear Sam, when God created the trees," Drewry explained, "He made sure they'd feel no pain."

She thought about the science lesson long after the children went inside to take their afternoon naps. *Millions of leaves—millions of scars,* she recalled, *yet the trees feel no pain at all. If only human hearts could be as sturdy!* Drewry sighed, recalling the way Chase had rejected her that day on the woodland path.

But enough self-pity! Drewry scolded herself. She'd made a promise to Matilda—and to herself—to stop whimpering about things that could never be and to start behaving like an adult. With a determined spring in her step, she led the children inside for their afternoon nap, then retrieved her latest book from her desk and brought it out to the terrace. There, beneath a fuzzy woolen coverlet, she read *Water Babies* and sipped warm apple cider from one of the big white mugs that hung on the wall above Matilda's stove.

She'd been sitting there in the sunshine for less than half an hour when the wind picked up. Crisp brown leaves skittered across the stone terrace floor, making soft scratching noises. The blanket she'd draped across her knees refused to stay tucked, and the pages of Charles Kingsley's wonderfully whimsical tale fluttered like bird wings.

Drewry looked beyond the hip-high stone wall that surrounded the terrace, shocked at the sudden bleakness of the fall
sky. Quickly she gathered her things to go inside, where it was
warm.

For the remainder of the afternoon, the wind whistled men-
acingly through the pines, bending the trunks of fragile willows
and birch in the woods beyond the lawn. Pinecones rolled hither
and yon, making Drewry think of the stories she'd read of the
nation's wild, wild West, where tumbleweeds bounced across the
landscape like huge round cages. The small woodland creatures
that generally scampered at the edge of the forest at this time of
day, foraging for food, were nowhere to be seen.

And all through Matilda's delicious dinner of roasted chicken
and baby potatoes, butter beans and beets, and popovers—Chase's
boyhood favorite—the wind soughed through the eaves of the
manor house. Bridget had just passed through the swinging door
that separated the kitchen from the dining room when a great
blast of air blew a pane from one of the windows. The chilly gust
doused all six candles in the chandelier, casting the dining room
into near darkness.

"Stay calm, everyone," Chase ordered, with a quiet air of
authority. "No need to panic."

Sam and Sally huddled with Bridget at the far end of the massive table as the tablecloth lifted like a giant white sail, overturning
water goblets and serving bowls. Silverware clattered against the
rose-patterned china. Milk, tea, and cider dripped onto the hardwood floor with a steady plop, plop, plop. Matilda and Drewry
gathered up the linen napkins and began to mop up the spills.

Chase darted from the room and returned moments later with
hammer, nails, and a piece of wood slightly larger than the missing
pane of glass. "Drewry," he called over his shoulder, "would you
come here and hold this for me while I fasten it in place?"

She hurried to oblige, not realizing how unnerving his nearness would be. Her heart beat erratically as she inhaled the pleasant masculine scent of him as he stooped over her to reach the bottom windowpane.

He'd removed his black dinner jacket and tie and rolled up the sleeves of his starched white shirt, exposing the muscles of his forearms. He worked quickly but efficiently, taking care not to damage the carved wood trimany more than necessary as he nailed the board over the offending hole.

"There. I believe that ought to do it," he announced, straightening to his full height.

It never ceased to amaze Drewry how it pleased Chase to work with his hands. His powerful, sinewy hands…

"You young'uns go on up to your rooms now and play for a spell," Matilda instructed. "Soon as Bridget an' me get this mess cleared up, we'll serve dessert." With that, the two women disappeared into the kitchen.

The children cowered near the door, obviously too frightened to climb the stairs alone—not as long as the mournful wailing of the wind continued outside.

"Chase," Drewry whispered near his ear, "would it be all right if the children joined me in the parlor instead? We could play backgammon or checkers until the storm passes."

Chase studied the worried faces of his son and daughter. "A splendid idea," he agreed in a conspiratorial whisper. "I'll join you there shortly." Then, to the children he said, "Perhaps if you ask her very politely, Drewry will play you a tune on the harpsichord."

Immediately, their faces brightened and they skipped off to wait in the parlor for the adults.

"I don't recall telling you that I could play the harpsichord."

He grinned. "Didn't have to tell me, I heard you playing when you thought no one was about." And with awave of the hammer, he headed for the kitchen. Just before he disappeared from sight, he winked...

...and left Drewry standing alone in her love-struck fog.

~

Drewry played until her fingers cramped and sang until her voice was hoarse, choosing lively tunes that would, she hoped, drown out the dreadful groaning of the wind.

Matilda had delivered dessert in the parlor, and the children were delighted to eat it, sitting on their feet at the polished mahogany serving table.

When the time came to tuck the children in for the night, Drewry promised to leave their bedchamber doors ajar, so the dim light of the hall lanterns would filter into their rooms.

Drewry understood their fears, for she'd experienced a restless agitation herself all evening, thanks to the ceaseless wind. Shortly after the children drifted off to sleep, the sky opened up and pelted the earth with sheets of icy rain and hailstones. Chase had retired to his library, and now, as she sat beside the fire in the downstairs parlor, she could hear his booted footsteps thudding back and forth across the carpeted floor. *If even Chase, who's always so controlled and calm, is on edge, it must mean that Mother Nature is brewing up something horrible.*

Sipping the tea Bridget had delivered only moments ago, Drewry shivered. She simply had to calm down. What sort of nanny was she if she couldn't remain composed on behalf of her young charges?

Hoping to lose herself in the pages of a book, she took up where she'd left off that afternoon. Then, coming to the conclusion of *Water Babies*, she rose to make another selection—Charles Dickens's *Great Expectations*—from a stack of books on the table. She expected to be mesmerized, as always, by the words of the popular author. Instead, lulled by the constant sighing of the wind, she snuggled deeper beneath the crocheted afghan on the divan and drifted off to sleep.

⟡

He hadn't meant to stand there gawking like a love-struck schoolboy, but then, he hadn't expected to find her curled up on the parlor couch like a contented kitten, either. She was a vision, lying there, Chase thought, her long lashes curving gently up from her rosy cheeks, her dark curls splayed out across the cushions like a chestnut fan. Draped in the afghan, she looked like the Italian painting of a guardian angel on display at the art museum during his last trip to New York.

Chase might have stood there, staring, until she woke, had a clap of thunder not startled him nearly out of his boots. He ran to the parlor window and parted the red velvet draperies. The storm showed no signs of abating any time soon.

His soy crop experiments would never withstand such a storm. And what of the delicate panes of glass in the hothouse? With this new dilemma creasing his brow, Chase thundered toward the foyer and grabbed his rain slicker from the hall tree, then dashed outside, slamming the heavy door behind him.

Drewry woke with a start and bolted upright. Heart pounding, something told her that the sound hadn't been thunder.

She stood alone in the hall for a moment, craning her ear to hear if Chase was still pacing in his library.

Silence.

Drewry tiptoed down the hall to peek into his private chamber.

Empty.

Perhaps he'd gone to the kitchen for a sip of water or a slice of pie.

No one was about.

The grandfather clock in the hall said nine forty-five...too early for Chase to retire, especially on a night like this.

And then, as surely as if an angel had whispered his whereabouts into her ear, Drewry knew where she would find him.

Grabbing her slicker from the hall tree, she ran outside, securing the door behind her. She'd find him in that field, no doubt, hovering over that ever-loving experiment of his. *What can he be thinking!* she ranted to herself, holding the hood of her raincoat over her head. *He could be struck by lightning, or felled by a tree branch, or....* Drewry didn't want to consider the possibilities.

And what are you thinking, Drewry Sheffield, she chided herself, *running after him this way?* The chances of finding him were slim, at best, what with the pounding rain and unrelenting wind. Why, in all likelihood, he'd have to send a search party out to rescue her before it was all over!

Still, she pushed on, peering through the darkness.

A bolt of lightning sliced the black sky, and she saw him, silhouetted by its silvery glare. She called to him, but a harsh clap of thunder drowned her out.

She'd have to go to him. He would chastise her, no doubt, but he'd chastised her before. She was becoming accustomed to his scoldings.

It seemed like hours instead of minutes before she reached him. He stood there, looking every bit as forlorn as he had on the night the Klan set fire to the other field. Following the direction of his gaze, she understood his anguish. This field, too, had been destroyed.

"Chase," she said, moving to stand alongside him, "come back to the house. I'll fix us a mug of warm milk."

Slowly, he turned to face her. "Are you mad? What are you doing out here?" he shouted above the din of the storm. "Why do you insist upon witnessing all my weakest moments?"

She'd come to expect more—better—from Chase. It unnerved her to see him behaving like a normal, flesh and blood man. How dare he stand there, assuming a defeated posture, sounding like a lost little boy! "I came," she added, her voice firm and strong now, "because I care about you, Chase Auburn!"

Chase took her in his arms and held her tight, then led her to a nearby shed that offered a little protection from the driving rain. "I'm sorry," he breathed against her hair, "so sorry to have shouted at you that way."

Drewry returned his hug. "It's all right," she soothed, comforting him as she would have one of the children. "It'll be all right. You'll see...."

She felt, rather than heard, his heaving sigh.

"I'm so grateful for you, Drewry. No matter how badly I've behaved or how cruelly I've spoken to you, you've been steadfast...a loyal friend."

He pushed back the hood of her raincoat, then gently cupped her face in his hands. "I'm a very fortunate man to have a friend I can share my troubles with—without fear of judgment or scorn."

Then, softly, so softly that she scarcely felt the pressure of his lips, Chase dropped a kiss on her forehead. "Yes, I'm a lucky man, and that's the truth."

Truth...truth...truth. The word echoed in her head, spinning and tumbling and leaving her stunned and breathless. This was the moment she had been dreading, the inevitable moment. It was time to tell Chase the truth.

"Let's go back now," she said, holding out her hand.

He took one last sad look at his ravaged field. Nodding, he put his hand into hers. "Yes, it's time," he agreed. "There's nothing we can do here. It's lost. But praise the Lord, everyone who means anything to me is safe."

On the way back to the house, she strained to make him hear her. Maybe it would be easier if she could say what she had to say out here. "There is something I must tell you, Chase."

"Another confession?" he called back with a grin.

Her heart thundered, louder it seemed, than the storm raging about them. "I'm not the person you think I am!"

He raised one dark brow. Just then a loud thunderbolt sounded, causing them to pick up their pace. "Don't try to talk right now," he shouted. "Whatever it is, it'll keep 'til we're back at the house."

They slogged on, half running now, each moment seeming an eternity to Drewry. Shedding their wet rainwear at the door, Chase led her to the parlor and summoned Bridget to bring them something hot from the kitchen.

"Now," he said, turning his full attention on Drewry, who sat sipping warm milk, "what's this about you not being Drewry Sheffield?"

"Well, I—I *am* Drewry Sheffield," she said uncomfortably, "but I'm not a nanny by trade."

Chase nodded. "Ah. So that explains it."

Drewry's brow furrowed. Why couldn't he simply be quiet and let her tell him what a lying deceiver she was? Why did he have to be so kind and warm, and make it so difficult to tell the truth?

"I thought the day we picked you up at the Richmond station you were a bit too...refined, shall we say, to be a servant girl. Smooth, soft hands. Lovely, well-fitted gowns. A true gentlewoman of breeding, with wit and intelligence."

She couldn't take any more! "Chase, please! I must tell you now, or I fear I'll never find the courage again!"

He chuckled softly. "All right. I'm sorry. Please, tell me all about your sinful past." He rose to put another log on the fire.

She took a deep breath. He thought she was joking. That whatever she planned to say could be dismissed as the silly ranting of an overwrought female mind. "I lied to you, Chase. I am not the woman the agency sent to care for Sally and Sam."

At that, Chase's head snapped around, his face betraying his confusion.

"I met a girl on the train," Drewry hurried on. "Her name was Suzie. *She* was to be your nanny."

"What became of her?" He returned to his chair and sank into the soft cushion with an expectant look on his face, as if waiting for her explanation to erase any doubt from his mind.

"She got off the train with a soldier she had met during the trip. They were to be married in Richmond."

Chase crossed his arms over his chest. "This is a fascinating story, Drewry. Do go on, please." He clamped his jaw and frowned, but he wasn't fooling Drewry. She saw that playful gleam in his eye dozens of times when he teased Sally and Sam.

He was making fun of her! But Drewry was determined to finish what she had begun. "She told me everything about you— that you would be wearing a blue silk scarf, that your two children would be with you, that you were successful and..."

"...and rich?"

"Yes." She heaved a sigh. What was the use? He probably wouldn't believe anything she said.'

"Ah-ha," he said thoughtfully. "I see." He steepled his fingers and studied her face. "Exactly why were you on that southbound train, Drewry?"

Go ahead! Tell it all! she shouted inwardly. *Show him what a worthless human being you really are!* "My uncle, James Sheffield, had been a loving guardian until he went off to fight in the War. He was wounded. After that..." *Don't stop now! Go on, or you'll lose your nerve!*

"When he came home," Drewry continued, "his wounds healed, but he took to drinking and playing cards in the saloon. He gambled away practically everything on the farm. And when he ran out of belongings—" she dropped her head, unable to meet his gaze. "He gambled me."

Chase inhaled sharply. "Gambled...*you?*"

Remembering her promise to Matilda, Drewry lifted her chin then and looked him in the eye. "That's right. Promised me to a horrible old man named Porter Hopkins. So, like a spoiled child, I took the coward's way out. I ran away from home. I didn't know where I'd go or what I'd do when I got there. I only knew I could never marry a man I didn't love."

Drewry cleared her throat, summoning the courage to finish her story. "I got on that train, and when I met Suzie and discovered she had no intention of keeping her bargain with you, I decided to take her place. I really thought it would solve all of our problems...." Her voice grew small and soft. "She'd get her handsome soldier, and you'd get your nanny."

There! She had done it. Drewry stared at the muddy toes of her boots, waiting for a storm of an entirely different kind to break over her head. Chase sat there for the longest time, saying nothing.

Finally, she looked up into his face. Never in all her days had she seen such rage, such fury, such outright anger....

Suddenly, he grabbed her shoulders and shook her. "Do you mean to say that..." He looked away, looked to heaven, looked back into her face, his countenance more fierce than before. "Why...I... of all the no good, despicable..."

She couldn't stand to hear any more. Drewry wrenched herself free and ran up the steps to the sanctuary of her room, leaving Chase alone.

Alone with her awful truth!

⌒

Drewry closed her door, and as the key clicked in the lock, it echoed the hollowness and desolation she felt inside. She slumped facedown onto her bed, and the nubby texture of the coverlet felt rough against her hot, tear-stained cheek.

So now he knew.

And now *she* knew that she'd lost him. It was only a matter of time before he demanded that she pack her things and leave.

He wanted no part of her, his rage had told her that much. He even had begun to call her names as he grasped her shoulders in the vise of his hands. Frightened by the disgust burning in those near-black irises, she had fled.

A strange sensation cloaked her: Instead of the self-pity she'd expected to feel, Drewry's heart ached for Chase. Her lies and deception had hurt him deeply, and he'd already suffered so many disappointments in life!

She thought of Suzie with bitterness. Had the fickle girl found happiness with her soldier? But it was hardly fair to blame the young woman. *She* hadn't misled Chase. The admission brought a fresh flood of tears. For the rest of her days, she would endure Chase's rejection as penance for her sin of dishonesty. Each lonely day that lay ahead would be torture. Having come so close to true love, she knew all too well what she would be missing—the joy of sharing a silly joke, the comfort of sharing one of life's traumas, the delight of sharing a kiss—all gone, forever.

And she had no one but herself to blame.

Yes, she had done the right thing in telling Chase the truth. Just as Jeb promised, the truth set her free. She was free now. Free from the awful burden of secrecy and shame.

Now that her conscience was clear in the sight of her Maker, perhaps in time, she could breathe easier. It was enough that she had obeyed her Lord. And even now, she dared to believe—to hope—that somehow, in His infinite mercy, He would bring something good of this heartbreak. God had forgiven her, of that Drewry was quite certain. Was it too much to hope that someday Chase, too, would find it in his heart to forgive her?

From his reaction downstairs in the parlor, that seemed highly unlikely.

It wouldn't be easy for him, she knew, to tell her that he couldn't have someone of questionable character caring for his children. She could spare him that, at least.

Drewry rose slowly and went to her desk, and, withdrawing a single sheet of stationery, sat down to write:

Magnolia Grange
October 2, 1868

Dear Mr. Auburn:

Due to certain unfortunate circumstances, it is with deepest regret that I must inform you that as of today, I can no longer remain in your employ. Please be assured that these circumstances have nothing whatsoever to do with you personally. I assume all responsibility for the occurrence which rendered our continued relationship untenable.

I have nothing but good things to report from my experience with you and your children. You have been more than a mere employer—you have been a friend of the highest caliber. It is with bitter regret that I confess—as I did tonight—that my own character has been found lacking.

Your high standards will, no doubt, assure you of retaining a more suitable young lady to serve as nanny to Miss Sally and Master Sam. Unless you find it intolerable for me to do so, I will, of course, remain in the household until that replacement has been secured. But I shall fully understand if you would prefer that I leave immediately.

I remain, in all sincerity, your friend,
Drewry Sheffield

With trembling hand, Drewry pen to its ink pot and gently blotted her letter. Once assured the ink was dry, she slipped the letter into a matching envelope and addressed it to Chase.

Heart pounding, she stepped into her houseshoes and silently made her way down the hall. Just as she expected, she saw the thin ribbon of light glowing from beneath his library door. Chase Auburn was a man of habit, to be sure. And habits were hard to break.

Honesty, she knew, was one of those habits.

Pausing briefly outside his door, Drewry closed her eyes and prayed. *Dear heavenly Father, I've tried my best to do your will. Now, all is in Your hands.* The simple words left her with a feeling of quiet assurance, as if God was waiting for just this prayer. Indeed, Drewry reasoned, if not a single sparrow fell to the ground without His notice, surely He knew about her aching heart and was working in her life now, no matter how bleak things seemed.

Holding her breath, she hunkered down, and, balancing herself, began to slide the envelope under the door as silently as possible. But the space beneath the door was slimmer than she reckoned and the letter wouldn't go in easily. It only half disappeared when the pocket doors whooshed open, the sudden force causing Drewry to lose her balance.

She flung out her arms to steady herself, but instead, she toppled sideways, cracking her head hard against the wooden door frame.

FIFTEEN

Drewry? Drewry! Are you all right, my love?"

What was that sound? Why was her head throbbing so? Then she remembered losing her balance, hitting her head....

She opened her eyes and found herself lying on the leather couch in Chase's library. Nearby, a lantern glowed brightly, and she drew comfort from the familiarity of the sight.

But there was something else. Was it...was it *love* she heard in Chase's voice?

She dared to look at him and found herself staring straight into dark eyes that seemed filled with shifting stars. Chase's eyes... Chase's voice...

"Thank God," he said, "you've come 'round."

She smiled weakly.

Gently, he wrung out a cloth and dabbed at her face. She gazed into his eyes, trying to read the expression hidden by the room's shadows.

"Does that feel better?" he asked, draping the cloth across her forehead.

She nodded.

Intently, he examined one eye, then the other. When he seemed satisfied that she hadn't suffered a concussion, he drew her to him and for a moment, enclosed her in the strong circle of his arms. When he turned her loose, Drewry looked longingly into his face, glowing and golden in the soft lamplight.

"It's never going to work, Drewry," he said softly, hanging his head.

Immediately, the pain of the previous hour came crashing in on her. She had assessed the situation correctly, after all, she realized sadly. He was rejecting her. His present ministrations were only further proof of his Christian kindness. He was concerned for her injury, but that was all.

"I understand," she whispered. "I plan to leave just as soon as you secure my replacement...."

When he looked up, Drewry saw tears glistening on his cheeks. Dazed, she reached up and traced their trail down his face.

"No, Drewry. You have it all wrong."

She heard deep undertones of anguish in his voice. "Wrong?" she echoed, hoping against hope.

"Completely. What I mean is—it's not going to work for you to hand in your resignation. I won't accept it."

"Oh?" she squeaked.

Chase let out a long, shuddering sigh. "What a fool I've been. When you confided your secret to me earlier, I...well, I'm ashamed to say I lost my temper."

Tenderly he repositioned the cloth on her forehead. "My dear, sweet Drewry. I'm sorry if I frightened you. It's just that I was so consumed with anger at your uncle for his brutal treatment of the woman I've come to love with all my heart. And I was angry at myself for not being there to protect you. My rage was so great, I was beside myself."

Drewry blinked, struggling to comprehend the meaning of his words. For months now, she'd yearned to hear these words; had he actually spoken them? Or was her mind playing tricks on her?

"Can you ever forgive me?"

If this was a dream, Drewry never wanted to wake up.

"Drewry, listen to me," Chase said softly, tucking a curl behind her ear, "you were thrust into such an impossible situation. Believe me when I say, from the bottom of my heart, there's nothing to forgive."

Nothing?

A wave of dizziness forced her to close her eyes. "I don't mind admitting that I'm afraid, Drewry," he said, his voice husky.

She opened her eyes. "Afraid? *You?*" It was almost laughable! "Afraid of what?"

His sigh echoed throughout the room. "First, I feared loving you. Now, I fear losing you, and I'd sooner lose an arm or a leg than have that happen. I think I've loved you from the first moment I set eyes on you at the Richmond station."

Drewry burrowed into the warm crook between his shoulder and neck, and shivered with delight as his arms tightened around her.

There was one thing she had to know, though. One thing that the rest of her world revolved around. One thing that only he could tell her.

"Chase?"

"Mmmm?"

"After knowing that I deceived you all these months, how will you ever trust me again?"

He gazed into her eyes with such intensity that she trembled.

"You proved your love for me when you told me your secret. I've been waiting so long for you to trust me enough to share it with me."

She blinked in astonishment. "Then…you *knew* I was hiding something? And didn't try to find out what?" Drewry gulped. "You could have hired a detective.…"

Chase chuckled. "Yes, I suppose I could have. But whatever it was, I wanted you to tell me about it, yourself."

Drewry sighed. "So many times I almost did. But I was afraid you'd hate me."

"So why, then, did you tell me tonight?"

"Because I love you too much to keep the truth from you for even one more hour."

Chase traced the outline of her jaw. "Well, there's the answer to your question, then. How can I *not* trust a woman who loves me enough to risk losing me by telling a painful truth?"

His voice poured over her like liquid music, soothing her, surrounding her, dissolving all her fears. In that moment, she felt warmer and safer than she ever felt before.

⌇

She stood in front of the oval mirror in her room and allowed Matilda to pin a white poinsettia in her hair. "You do make a lovely bride, Miss Drew," she said, meeting Drewry's eyes in the mirror. "Mr. Chase be one lucky fella to be gettin' a wife like you."

"Thank you, Matilda." Drewry studied her reflection, seeing the flush of excitement in her cheeks. "And I'm lucky, too."

"Not lucky," Bridget corrected her. "Blessed."

The girl so rarely spoke that the mere sound of her voice stunned Matilda and Drewry into silence. After a moment, Drewry grasped the girl's hand. "You're so right, Bridget. Luck has nothing to do with it. It was the good Lord who brought Chase and me together."

"And 'tis the Lord who will *keep* you together," Bridget confirmed with a nod.

Drewry and Matilda exchanged amused glances. "Seems our gal here know as much about the Good Book as anyone," Matilda said, grinning.

"You'd best be gettin' downstairs, Miss," the Irish girl interrupted, adjusting Drewry's long, flowing veil. "Pastor Tillman has arrived, and the guests have gathered in the chapel."

The weather turned unseasonably warm. Even in Richmond, temperatures in the seventies were almost unheard of in December. Drewry knew she had God to thank for that, too.

She tugged at the long, snug sleeves of her white velvet gown, then held them out so that Matilda could fasten the tiny pearl buttons on each cuff. She secured her mother's cameo at the high stand-up collar of the dress, then picked up her bouquet, which Bridget had fashioned of red roses, white poinsettias, and fresh greenery from Chase's hothouse.

"Well, I'm as ready as I'm ever going to be," she said, her voice trembling.

"Let's go on down, then!" Matilda said.

Out front, Claib was waiting with the carriage. He had polished the chassis until it gleamed like a black mirror. He cut quite a dashing figure in his long-tailed morning suit, and Drewry told him so.

Bending low at the waist, he swept a gloved hand in front of him. "Your carriage awaits, m'lady," he said, mimicking Pastor Tillman's English butler.

The sounds of laughter and chatter grew louder as Drewry, Bridget, and Matilda rode across the field toward the chapel. "They're here!" she heard a woman shout. "Start the music!" a man hollered. "The bride has arrived!"

As the four-piece string ensemble began to play—*something by Beethoven*, she thought—Drewry stood at the end of the path that led to the tiny chapel, marveling at its festive seasonal decorations. The red berries of the holly that trimmed the roof winked merrily at her, and the soft garland of green that trimmed the walls filled the air with the fresh, clean scent of pine. Inside, massive arrangements of white poinsettias and fresh evergreens banked the altar where Chase would be waiting.

As Drewry remained at the back of the church, ready for the bridal processional to begin, Bridget and Matilda, wearing new frocks, found their places in the Auburn pew. Young Sally took up her position, too, prepared to sprinkle rose petals along the path that her new mother's high-topped white boots would take. Beside Sally was little Sam, carrying the white satin pillow that cushioneda wide gold band. Squirming in his new suit, he grinned up at Drewry.

Scanning the church filled with family and friends, Drewry spotted Uncle James. Beside him, his lovely Joy sitting between her fiancé and her brother-in-law to be, Jeb Sheffield. Missy sat on Jeb's right. Drewry's family, who turned in their seats like unruly schoolchildren to catch a glimpse of the bride, beamed their approval, and she blew them a kiss.

At that moment, the processional began and Pastor Tilton, followed by Chase, emerged from a small room at the side of the church to take their places at the altar.

Chase—resplendent in black suit and tie and starched white shirt, his dark hair gleaming, his eyes searching for hers. Chase—the object of all her hopes and dreams, the promise soon to be fulfilled. Chase—God's special gift to her....

Catching her eye, he mouthed "I love you."

"I love you, too," she mouthed back.

And that, she thought, *is no bluff!*

ABOUT THE AUTHOR

A prolific writer, Loree Lough has more than seventy books, sixty short stories, and 2,500 articles in print. Her stories have earned dozens of industry and Reader's Choice awards. A frequent guest speaker for writers' organizations, book clubs, private and government institutions, corporations, college and high school writing programs, and more, Loree has encouraged thousands with her comedic approach to "learned-the-hard-way" lessons about the craft and industry.

For decades, Loree has been an avid wolf enthusiast, and she dedicates a portion of her income each year to efforts that benefit the magnificent animals. She splits her time between a home in the Baltimore suburbs and a cabin in the Allegheny Mountains. She shares her life and residences with a spoiled pointer named Cash and her patient, dedicated husband, Larry, who has supported her writing and teaching endeavors throughout the years.

Loree loves hearing from her readers, so feel free to write her at loree@loreelough.com. To learn more about Loree and her books, visit her Web site at www.loreelough.com.